I0637802

One Life

Or

The Lives

of

Chester Knowles

a novel

by

Stephen Baum

Copyright ©2011 by Stephen Baum

ISBN: Softcover   978-0-9886-1180-1
             Ebook   978-0-9886-1180-1

All rights reserved. No part of this book may be reproduced or transmitted in any form or by any means, electronic or material, without permission in writing from the copyright owner.

This is a work of fiction. Names, characters, and incidents are either the product of the author's (twisted) imagination or are used fictitiously. Any resemblance to any actual persons or events is entirely coincidental.

This book was printed in the United States of America

The reincarnations of the soul are endless. For it (the soul) is eternal and its manifestations are beyond reckoning.

Upanishads. Chapter 37

When you die you're dead. Six feet under. All that stuff about heaven and hell is a crock of shit.

Rupert Knowles, Chester's grandfather

The Will

This is my last will and testament. I, Chester Knowles, hereby declare myself to be of sound mind and body (which, by the way, would have to be a worthless statement in a court of law. After all, how many psychotics walk right up and confess right away to being crazy? So, let's just assume that I'm all right in the head, OK?). My body, though, may be another story. My doctor at Kaiser told me last week that he doesn't like the way my heart sounds (whatever that means!). Also he said that my cholesterol is too high. He's sending me for an electrocardiogram, as well as some other tests. He described me as a type "B" individual, which means that I don't worry too much. Hah! Why do you think I'm writing this? Because I'm relaxed? Maybe I'm B+ or A-. Anyway, this is my Will and Testament:

To my family I leave all my worldly possessions. Everything in the house, all the bank accounts, the pension plan, the mutual fund from work. There's a life insurance policy for a few thousand dollars at work too. It's separate from the pension, so you'll have to remind them about it. Talk to Cindy at personnel. All these monies, whatever they're worth, whatever they total, are to go to my wife Marsha (who I also hereby designate as the executor of this will) and to my two daughters, Laura and Vicki. Actually, everything goes directly to Marsha anyway, but I do request that Marsha put aside twenty thousand dollars in separate trust funds for each of the girls. My paintings and sculptures try to sell. Maybe they'll fetch a better price when I'm dead. Sometimes that happens.

My clothes give to the Salvation Army; they're a good organization, and they'll come to pick them up. The rest, the books, the tapes, the tools in the garage, the old records do what you want. Ask Stan to come take what he wants, and Tommy and Bill can also take what they want. The rest, Marsha, just get rid of.

All the bankbooks and papers are in the top left drawer of the dresser. Call Mike if you need help with any of that. The house is in both our names, so there shouldn't be any problem with that.

So that's it. I give you my love. It is yours eternally. Whatever happens, my love would be eternal, I can feel that aspect of it. It makes a certain sense. Anyway, who knows? If you're reading this, I'm already a goner. So good-bye. The funeral make simple. A plain wooden box. And no eulogies with everybody talking nonsense about me. I hate all that crap.

So, that's it. So long. See ya in the next life.

Love,

Chester Knowles,
July 14, 1996

The Inquest

The above document was found by Chester's wife Marsha several days after his death - or presumed death. The hospital's insurance agent likened it to "a suicide note", but the judge at the inquest, which was held just twenty-eight days after the death, just chuckled. The note was recognized for what it was: a simple holographic "last will and testament" written, as it turned out, just two weeks before Chester Knowles' sudden illness/disappearance.

The death was "presumed", but in fact there was no doubt about it in anyone's mind. Not even the insurance agent's! He afterwards confided as much to Marsha's lawyer. Chester Knowles had suffered a severe heart attack on the 28th of July, and had been in "very critical condition" in the Intensive Cardiac Care Unit of Cedars Sinai Medical Center in Los Angeles for eight days. He had been in a complete coma for all of that time.

But somehow, inexplicably, he had managed to get up and out of his hospital bed (the rails were found lowered), and then somehow to make it out of the "monitored and supervised" intensive care unit in the middle of the night (sometime between 1:00 and 1:20 A.M.), and then to slip outside - totally unnoticed by anyone, totally undetected.

He disappeared. He simply vanished. Hospital personnel, and later the police (the police were contacted at 6:45 AM), purportedly conducted a "thorough and exhaustive search". After twenty-eight days, at the request of an exhausted family - and with the intervention of an assemblyman from Sacramento - the conclusion was reached by the Court that Chester had died, and a death certificate was issued. Several bodies had been found in the Los Angeles River downtown, but they were damaged beyond identification. It was possible his was one of them. One of the male bodies had a matching blood type, and, what with all the noise in the newspapers and on the local news channels, the police speedily had the body delivered to the funeral home for a closed-coffin memorial ceremony and burial.

In issuing the death certificate, the Court's overriding consideration (aside from the political pressure) was Chester's illness. His heart attack had been a severe and sudden coronary. He had lain motionless on the so-called "edge of death" for eight days. Such a patient, attested several doctors at the inquest, could not possibly live for more than several hours without medical supervision and life supports. Thus, the Court concluded that Chester Knowles had died. The hospital administrators were naturally very embarrassed and put out by the incident. They feared a massive lawsuit for malpractice and negligence. Indeed, the wife's lawyer was already preparing to file suit.

The Funeral

The funeral, a simple ceremony as per Chester's request, was held on August 31. It was a hazy L.A. morning, full of glare. The 405 freeway was thick with traffic. Long creeping lines of sedans, various sports utility vehicles and small trucks stretched up the Sepulveda pass. At ten AM, it wasn't rush hour traffic. It was simply the constant, overbearing crush of humankind. Every year there were more cars, more people, more construction. The concrete freeway lined the canyon floor. High-power electric cables spanned across the hillsides. The chaparral, the sandy mountain landscape, the bushes, the birds and small animals - whatever natural beauty that remained - was living on borrowed time.

Marsha Knowles sat silently in the backseat of the air-conditioned Cadillac hearse, flanked by her two daughters, Laurie and Vicki, who were dressed in new, stiff dresses, and who both looked straight ahead in silence. Chester's brother Stan sat up front with the driver. After several attempts to engage the girls in conversation, Stan had grown quiet, too.

He looked at the road ahead, the lines of cars, the exit signs for streets in the Valley - Burbank Blvd, Victory Blvd, Sherman Way, Roscoe Blvd. - and he shifted in his seat. They were going to the cemetery. For an "internment" - what a word, internment - of Chester, goddammit. Chester had been taken from them. It felt like a knife wound in the stomach, the sadness of it. Stan didn't want to think about wondering why. Later, when he got back home. Later, he'd have a chance to think. Right now there was this funeral, this internment, to take care of. And Chester's family needed taking care of.

Poor Marsha was out in left field. She'd been this way all week. It was as if she didn't hear correctly. She was numb. She didn't respond to anything he said to her, and he had already stopped trying with her.

So, it was a good thing that he, Stan Knowles, was there. He knew that. He knew that he was a capable and rational person, someone who could get things done. And it was his duty and responsibility, he thought, to try to help, to salvage - to "keep going" was the way he thought of it - what was left of his brother's family. And especially to spare the poor girls from as much sorrow as possible. It was wrong to be thinking of oneself. The more Stan turned it over in his mind, the more Marsha's behavior was making him angry. What about the girls? Wasn't it hard enough on them? Wasn't it going to be even harder in the coming months? Why couldn't she think of them?

But Marsha sat motionless, looking out the window at the god-awful 405 freeway. "Counting the cars on the New Jersey Turnpike," Stan muttered to himself, quoting the old Simon and Garfunkel song..... "Let us be lovers, we'll marry our fortunes together." Yes, that was how the song went. Stan thought of Chester. They used to sing those old Simon and Garfunkel tunes all the time. Up in their bedroom. Stan played the guitar, Chester the drums. Tommy Shea, Chester's friend, used to play guitar too. They had studied those Simon and Garfunkel records laboriously. And then Chester had insisted they learn the Everly Brothers' songs. His argument was that if they played Simon and Garfunkel, then they must also play the Everly's. They were "prerequisite" he said. Stan remembered how Tommy had teased Chester about the use of the word prerequisite. Tommy had joked that they were only playing music, not getting a college degree. But Chester, God bless him, responded with an even more extreme stance. He asserted that if Simon and Garfunkel were a college degree, then the Everly's were like a high school diploma.

They were easy enough songs, but Chester was never satisfied with their renditions. Chester was a perfectionist. Other people didn't see him that way because he was so easy going. But when it came to matters of art and taste, Chester was a little tyrant. He would listen to the Everly Brothers and exclaim: "Isn't that incredible, Stan? We are miles and miles from that!"

Yes, miles and miles, and years and years, thought Stan, as the road continued to move by. Stan eased his big body back in the seat, and smiled. A few tears rolled down his cheek. Vicki, from the back seat, noticed immediately. She began crying too. Stan reached in his trouser pocket and found his pack of Juicy Fruit and gave the girls each a stick.

"Say, girls, have you ever heard the Everly Brothers? No? You either, Laurie? Oh well, you have to hear them sometime. Your father used to love them.

"Why? I don't know why..... Well, maybe I do know why. It's just hard to put it into words...... Anyway, he used to like 'em. They were different from today's music. Slower and sweeter with very nice harmonies. They were just beautiful. I think that's why he likes them so much... I mean why he liked them so much. Because they created something beautiful.......Yeah, well.......oh....uh.....OK, girls. Here, we are."

They had arrived at the cemetery, and the big car was slowly ascending a curved road. The gravesite was near the top of a hill. After waiting for some trucks to back out, the driver edged forward, and parked the hearse alongside the open grave. Stan got out to open the door for Marsha and the girls, and they lined themselves up along the roadside, as the driver and pallbearers, who seemed to appear from nowhere, slowly eased the coffin out of the hearse. Marsha's long, black hair hung limply onto her shoulders. Her slender body seemed to sag and merge with the ground.

For several moments she stood motionless. And then, as if she drew her sorrow up from the earth, she raised her head toward the grey sky, and released a chilled and anguished howl. She rushed past Stan, and threw herself onto the ground like a bug. She scrambled on her knees along the asphalt road, lurching at the wooden casket. Despite the efforts of Stan and several of the women, she clung pathetically to the brass handles, as the pall bearers tried to carry the coffin to the gravesite. She wouldn't let go, wouldn't tear herself away from the wooden box - which contained the remains, the "presumed" remnants, of the body of her husband. Of Chester. Her mother and sister eventually grabbed hold of her. Stan led the girls to the other side of the lawn. Who needed an embarrassment at this time?

The family was plain Presbyterian folk who weren't accustomed to such outbursts. One of Chester's cousins, a middle-aged woman with a recently-conferred PhD. in family therapy, announced to everyone in a loud voice that it was a "part of the grieving process". "This is a part of the grieving process, everybody. Don't worry."

A large congregation - over a hundred people - stood uncomfortably along the hillside gravesite. There were people from work, there were neighbors, friends, family, even some strangers who had read of the affair in the newspaper. Marsha's outburst had frightened them, and they now began to mutter and chatter nervously. They remarked to one another about the size of the crowd. "A tribute to Chester". The words "forty-four", Chester's age, could be heard repeatedly among the murmurings. The words "hospital" and "police" could also be discerned.

The minister, a tall, young, blond-haired but dark-bearded man, with a narrow face, and strange, nervous brown eyes, walked over to a makeshift wooden podium. He began with the standard,

"Friends, we are gathered here today.........."

Marsha began to moan.

"Friends, we are gathered here today to pay our last respects to our dear departed husband, father, son, brother, and very dear friend, Chester Knowles. It is not an easy task." Here he paused.

"While I myself never met Chester, I have talked quite a bit about him with his brother Stan as well as with several other family members... and I have the clear impression of a man who was deeply and truly loved. A man who was loved, and who loved as well. A man who lived in the service of our Lord Jesus Christ, a man who tried to do good, a man whose goodness reached out to all of us."

Here he paused again. He looked out over the assembly, folded his hands in a deliberate manner, and slowly examined a piece of paper that rested on the podium.

"He was a good man. A good father to his daughters Vicki and Laurie. A good husband to his wife Marsha. A devoted brother to his brother Stan. A good co-worker, a good neighbor................"

"Enough already!" screamed Marsha, "Leave him alone already!"

"Well," answered the young preacher, turning from the podium to face her directly, "I hadn't intended to......."

"No, of course not, Father. I'm sorry........ And I thank you for your sermon," she continued in a voice remarkably cool and level. "But, could you please stop?"

After several nervous glances and non-verbal exchanges between the preacher and Stan, the preacher read the eighteenth Psalm, walked back to his car, and the large crowd began to disperse.

The driver drove them directly home. They got out of the big Cadillac. Marsha took Stan's hands in her own:

"Stan, I'm asking you to please forgive me. I know you could say there were extenuating circumstances, and that I could make excuses for myself. But there is no excuse for the way I acted.... And I don't care if the girls hear it either, Stan. They know it, too. I acted terribly. And I need to apologize to you. Most of all to you, Stan. Because........"

And here she broke off in tears, as Stan wrapped his arms around her and rocked her gently, as they stood on the sidewalk alongside the car, the girls looking on uncomfortably, impatiently.

"OK, Stan. I'll call you. You go back home. I'll be all right. Sandy'll be coming over later. You go home. You have a long drive."

Marsha slowly turned and walked up the driveway. The girls in their starched dresses followed behind like goslings.

She unlocked the door to their home. The key fit roughly but then turned easily in the new brass tumbler Chester had installed only a few months before. It had been only a few months, but it seemed like an eternity.

Marsha remembered the day well. It had been a Sunday. A beautiful, sunny day. Chester had needed to borrow a special drilling attachment from Billy next door. Poor Chester had worked all afternoon on the repair, which he had estimated would take "maybe an hour". Marsha softly pressed her forehead to the door. She remembered she had yelled at him for making a mess, but Chester had shrugged her off. Shreds of wood were strewn all over the carpet. His tools and drill bits lay scattered on the doorstep. He had barely heard her, so concerned had he been about "the measurements". Marsha smiled wearily. Chester was always going on about "the measurements". Slowly she pushed open the big red door, and entered the foyer - which was crowded with fading bouquets and floral arrangements.

Marsha paused. Laurie leaned her head on Marsha's hip. Condolence cards, with their photos of flowers and crucifixes, stood half-opened on the mantelpiece in two long rows. They looked like children in line in a schoolyard. Waiting quietly for something. The odor of faded, dying flowers filled the hallway. Marsha stood transfixed. The girls waited alongside her, conscious of the silence, afraid to make a noise. The silence buzzed in the house. The absence of Chester was a fact.

Finally, Vicki squeezed past Marsha, and trudged up the stairs. Laurie followed several steps behind. Neither turned to look back at Marsha. It had been a long day and Chester was no longer with them in this harshly quiet house.

The next day, the girls returned to school. Marsha drove them, and then came back to the house to cry. This became the routine. The house became a bit run-down looking. Stan came down from Sacramento after two weeks, though. He told Marsha that he was staying until she got herself in order. He enrolled her in a health club, and insisted she go to a therapist. He helped her clean the house and put Chester's things "in order".

He met several times with Marsha's lawyer, whom he did not like, but who seemed to be advocating well for Marsha and the girls' interests. The hospital had already offered to settle out of court, a course which Stan favored, but the lawyer argued that they would get a better deal later on. Stan commented that this new breed of lawyer was "even worse than the old breed". But Marsha seemed to like the young fellow for some reason, and that bothered Stan, too. After a week he returned to Sacramento with two cardboard boxes of Chester's old phonograph records, some of their Dad's old tools, and a stack of drawings and cuttings. Marsha and the girls sank deeply into a quiet, silent sort of life. Marsha became very involved with the girls' schoolwork, and gradually she became more active. Her appetite improved. She particularly enjoyed the exercise at the health club. She went every day after she dropped the girls off at school. She cut her hair short. She began to look younger, stronger. However, she resisted going to the therapist. She wasn't ready yet, she told Stan on the phone.

"Not yet, Stan. Not yet", she pleaded.

"But Marsha, it's been three months already....."

"That's what I mean. It's only been three months! And.... well...OK, Stan, I'll go see this Dr. Gold of yours. I know. I know he's gone. Chester's gone.
And I know I have to take care of myself and....."

"Life goes on, Marsha."

"That's right, Stan, but....."

"You know, Marsha? You know, I still kind of wonder where he is. Where Chester is."

"Yeah, me too."

Waking Up

Chester Knowles returned to himself five months after his "death".

He was not dead. He wasn't even sick. He felt just fine. He felt like himself.

However, he was no longer "himself". His body was a totally different one! Chester could not understand how this could be, nor could he understand very much of anything.

He knew his name, but it meant nothing; there was no significance or moment to this knowledge; he had no history; and as a result he had no real personality. He knew that his name was Chester Knowles, but he didn't know what kind of person Chester Knowles was supposed to be. He knew where he was, but had no idea how he had gotten there. He knew that he was alive, but he also knew that he had died. It was a problem to know how to behave. What to think, what to do, what to feel! He was a tabula rosa, and he struggled to recall how he knew that term, tabula rosa. It was something he had learned at school - he remembered a lot of things about school. He remembered many things now, the memories were almost like emotions that swept over him.

He was just now beginning to recall things and reconstruct memories about his life - and about what had happened to him. He still wondered how he had gotten to be where he was: in a small wooden cabin above the snow line at the Sequoia National Park in central California.

Only this past week his memory, his mental faculties, had begun to return to him. He could now visualize himself

- as if in a dream - a movie flashback or dream sequence. It was a picture of himself, Chester A. Knowles, in a hospital bed:

Gripping the clear plastic wires in his palms and then, with a splendid decisiveness, yanking them forcefully out of the spigots - yes, they were miniscule spigots - that were embedded under the skin of his arms. These were his arms, his own arms (he remembered saying that to himself: "these are my own arms!") and, as he sat up on the edge of the hospital bed, he felt a rush of awareness or blood flow like some warm light to the top of his head. His bare feet dangled in the air off the edge of the bed. He was no longer connected to the pumping machines. Energy surged and tingled throughout his body - a gratitude to be free from the wires, and free from the medication that had been dripped into his blood continuously the past eight days.

He felt the energy in his limbs, in his veins and capillaries, as he sat on the edge of the bed. His whole body tingled strangely. He felt glad to be dying. He brought his palms together in prayer. Just as he began to say "Our Father Who Art in Heaven", just as the words were passing silently over his lips, the idea flashed though his mind or heart that he needed to get out of this hospital if he wanted to live any longer. Suddenly he had a choice: he could spend his last moments in prayer - and the prayer would be his last act on earth - or he could spend his last moments in trying to be alive.

He reached over to pick up the blanket that was folded on the plastic chair alongside his bed. Grasping a door jamb, he pulled himself upright. He was standing. He stepped into the empty hallway. To his right was the nurse's station. Three or four nurses, dressed in white and powder blue, were gathered around a computer screen playing Tetris. Chester recognized the familiar colored cubes of the falling blocks game; they used to play Tetris at his job too.

He turned left toward a sign that said Exit. It was as if his bare feet were drawn forward by the cold, clean feeling of the linoleum floor. He pushed on the Exit door and stepped onto a chilled metal grating.

An endless stairwell of steps and railings greeted him with a gust of cold air. The stench of mildew rose from the stairwell and passed over him. It gave him the shakes. Nonetheless, he began to descend the staircase one cold, cruel step at a time. After perhaps fifteen minutes he reached the bottom. The stairs ended in the basement. The exit door would not yield when he leaned his shoulder against it. It was with difficulty that he turned the doorknob, for his hands were trembling. He unfolded the hospital blanket and draped it over his shoulders. He peered down the long, grey, concrete corridor. Water pipes hung suspended from the ceiling; they seemed to extend forever. Chester thought he had arrived in hell. The steps had brought him to hell. He staggered alongside the concrete wall, turned a corner, and slammed against a wall of grey, metal lockers. His neck and face were dripping sweat, and he was shivering, seized by the chills. He pulled the blanket more tightly around his shoulders. Chester wished to God that he didn't have to die in hell. He began to pray again: "Our Father Who Art in Heaven...."

He remembered praying alongside the lockers. He remembered reading a hospital bulletin board with postings of job openings and safety regulations. He remembered staggering around the basement hallways, saying to himself over and over, "This place is hell, and I must find a way out."

He remembered the feeling of desperation and the long search for a way out, the frantic walking and stumbling down the long concrete corridors - but more than that he couldn't recall. In his mind, in his remembering, he was stuck at the point where he had been stuck! Although he tried again and again, he couldn't remember how he had gotten out of the hospital building, or how he had gotten out of Los Angeles. Or how he had gotten up into these wonderful, snow-covered mountains.

Another puzzle was that he had $55,000 in 100 dollar denominations in a manila envelope - which he kept in his backpack. How did he get that money? How could it be that he have such a big sum of money and not know how it had come into his hands? It was a lot of money after all. Everything in his life, all the contents of his mind, was a great puzzlement. How could it all be, and how had the time passed? He now considered that it could even be that these missing months of his life, from the summer until the winter, had been spent in this way: he had been puzzling over what exactly had transpired. Perhaps he had spent all this time just trying to figure things out!

But now he had come to accept that he (Chester A. Knowles, he himself, his person, his personality, the man he was, the man he was trying to remember, the man he was supposed to be) he himself was only a phantom, an abstraction of the mind. A spirit, a ghost. Chester liked the word phantom, though. He called himself a phantom, and smiled. He was a phantom. A phantom of someone else's imagination. A phantom, even, of his own imagination. And once he had made that step, once he saw things in this way, life became easier. Indeed life was now quite wonderful to him.

He awoke in his cabin when the morning light filtered through the white curtains of the window. The light was bright because of all the snow. The light was nearly white. He remembered someone telling him that Jewish people have a prayer that they say upon waking: "Thank you, Lord, for bringing me back to the world of the living."

He sat on the edge of the bed and reached for his snow pants and boots. Turning on the electric heater he entered the little bathroom. As he brushed his teeth, he studied the mirror. Each time he looked in the mirror he was awe-struck by the man who gazed back at him, right into his own eyes. Although he knew that this person was himself, it wasn't actually himself. He looked like someone else, an older man with white hair. A long, drawn, dreamy face - with a grey beard. Chester decided to shave right there and then. He had already bought the necessary shaving equipment the evening before down in Visalia. Slowly, he wet his face and beard with hot water and soap. Then he applied piles of clean, white Noxzema shaving cream. Carefully, he tried the new razor, a Gillette Trac II. It was rough going, but after several applications of the shaving cream, and a change of blades, a fresh, red, boyish face emerged. Strangely, the new face matched the white hair. It was a splendid face with sharp cheekbones, a long, sunburned nose, and an easy smile. It was a thinner, more angular face than his old face.

He smiled into the new face in the mirror. It was funny, but his eyes were the same color, which was interesting. He leaned forward to examine the grey-blue eyes, the left larger and quite different from the right. He played with the possibility that he could discover who he was if only he could look deeply enough into his own eyes. "The eyes are the windows to the soul". Where had he heard that one?

But it was no use. It was a childish game, he decided, to examine oneself. It was a logical contradiction. A stupid thought. A mirror could reflect upon itself endlessly. It would still be an illusory reflection. And the light would be wasted, or would it? And thoughts would reflect upon themselves in a similar way. Thinking so much makes me a fool, too. So, I'm foolish, I'm stupid. Well, that's OK, too.

He dried his face with the skimpy, motel towel, put on his ski jacket, and woolen stocking hat. He readied his leather gloves and slipped on his backpack, which held the

$55,000 envelope, as well as his personal effects (he had become intensely attached to his personal effects, his "things"). When he opened the door and stepped out onto the little, wooden porch, the cold wind struck his raw face. He turned up the hood of his jacket, and pulled the drawstring tight. The sun was still behind the trees, and the snow gave off a glow of reflected, or reverberated, white light.

The park cafeteria was the only place to eat for miles around. The food was dismal. For a decent meal you needed to trek 20-odd miles down the hill - through the snow no less. You needed to have a ride. Chester still had not gotten accustomed to the cafeteria food. He ordered French toast and coffee (the coffee wasn't so bad). He carried his tray to a table in the corner.

The big, high-ceilinged, wood-paneled dining room was nearly empty. The hotel staff and park rangers had already eaten. It was quiet in the park this time of year. You had to be "some kind of crazy", as one of the rangers liked to say, to have made it up to the top of the hills this time of year. There were some cross-country skiers. There were the occasional teams of winter backpackers with their truckloads of expensive equipment. Sometimes a group of Europeans or Japanese tourists arrived to witness the famous sequoias in the snow. Or maybe they simply took their vacations in the winter. Who knew? They were pleasant and polite people generally. Often, surprisingly often, they would attempt to engage Chester in conversation, and, as they were foreigners, the conversation was typically simple and easy for Chester to handle. He found that he could never understand them clearly or satisfactorily, but that, in the end, it didn't matter much. As for why they chose to visit in the winter, Chester could never determine.

He himself had also come for no particular reason. At least he could remember no reason. His mind was pretty much a blank on that score. He only knew that he had arrived here on a tour bus - a few months before the snow started to fall. He felt now as if he might stay forever.

The large dining hall was a pleasant place to sit, and, as he ate, Chester patiently observed the minor goings-on: the small group of European tourists seated across the room, the kitchen help scurrying about, the hotel employees chatting with the cashier. He could easily become absorbed in watching the way events seemed to spill out in front of him. Like some movie, each scene, each event followed the other. There was a pattern and a rhythm. To align his senses and feelings to the flow was a pleasurable endeavor. The events were connected in some way, and he was drawn to discern the connections. The law of cause and effect lay beneath the surface of everything. Theoretically, everything could be explained. But in reality nothing was clear. The more he thought about things, the less clear they became.

The only thing that remained clear was the rhythm, the pace, the pattern. The law of cause and effect was imposed by people, and since every man's and every woman's perceptions and logic were different, then the law of cause and effect was a bit of a phantom too.

The question that obsessed him was what was really happening? Could the law of cause and effect, as well as everything else, be a product of his mind? Could he himself be a product of his mind? What was really happening? He didn't know, and had already come to the conclusion that he most likely never would. But there was a persistent need in him, a compulsion, to make sense of the world. It could easily become overwhelming: this constant struggle to rationalize and understand everything. Chester knew that if he got caught up in it, he would exhaust himself and ruin the whole day. It was OK to watch, but the rationalizing, the trying to understand everything, was something he knew he must avoid. He had learned that already. The rationalizing started as a sort of game and then it took over your mind.

The group of Europeans - young people, cross-country skiers probably - were drinking coffee and discussing something with a sense of urgency. One of them stood up, dramatically thrust his hands into his bulky ski gloves, and started to wave and flap his arms. One of the young men at the table declared something several times - in German or Dutch, Swedish perhaps. With each proclamation he slapped his palm on the table, as if he were wielding a gavel. In his mind Chester dubbed this man "the judge". Then they all became silent, each one avoiding eye contact, seemingly oblivious of the others. That was an interesting configuration, thought Chester. There were three men and three young women. After a while, with no perceived signal, they all rose to leave - except for one of the women, who remained seated with her long legs stretched out on the wooden floor, her arms folded across her chest - in a pose of defiance. Another verbal exchange ensued. The others gesticulated and chatted nervously in their language. But the young woman refused to budge. She addressed them in a clear, cold, cutting tone. "Geit schoen", or something like that.

And that was it. Wordlessly now they now exited, stomping noisily in their large, brand-new boots on the wooden floor directly in front of Chester's table, and then out the door to his right - into the lobby where their voices could again be heard in heated Germanic argument. The young woman remained seated where she was. Her eyes were on the tops of her boots, her arms still clasped across her chest, her legs stretched out on the wooden floor in front of her. Then slowly, and very deliberately, she lifted her gaze across the room to look directly at Chester. Her green eyes - he could identify their color even from across the room - glared at him.

Chester smiled weakly and turned back to his breakfast plate; he felt embarrassed. It was curious to watch people, entertaining even, but it was unwise to get involved. Chester felt at home only amongst the trees and the bushes, the birds and small mammals of the forest. In the world of nature he could intuit directly to the feel of things. But in the world of men and women the task was too difficult, and he needed to maintain a distance. Even if people were just another natural phenomenon, another species to study, another aspect of the world, they were a terribly complicated aspect. Human beings seemed to defy the laws of nature. Chester had learned to avoid situations that were upsetting. It was difficult enough just to remember who he was and what needed to be done each day. Being a phantom wasn't easy. Things were much simpler and easier, he found, if he could avoid people as much as possible.

All the time he had been at the cabin he had spoken very little, and only on a superficial level, to the hotel staff as well as some of the tourists and park rangers. Just pleasantries: talk about the weather, nothing personal, nothing from the heart. Everyone was very pleasant, very courteous. Although initially puzzled by his long residence at the cabin, the people in the park had grown accustomed to the white-haired man who did not ski, or hunt, or photograph - who didn't seem to do much of anything but walk around in the woods and keep to himself. Several of the rangers, themselves lonely and hungry for conversation, had been quite friendly. They would offer him rides "down the hill" to Visalia, invite him to come over for drinks in the evening. Chester typically refused.

However, one of the rangers, an older man named Harry, had insisted a few weeks before that Chester learn to play bridge (they needed him for the fourth hand). Before the others arrived Harry had walked him through the rules of bidding and playing the hand. Chester struggled for most of the evening. But abruptly, in the middle of the bidding, (he was holding three aces and three kings) Chester recalled that he already knew how to play bridge. He used to play bridge with Marsha, and Tommy and Rosie. Their faces came to him. They were with him - almost physically. He remembered them all clearly, but most particularly he remembered the joy of the game - the feeling of it. With moist eyes he peered down at his hand - and grinned. He was holding a "slam". His partner had opened with two diamonds - which was Chester's only weak suit.

"C'mon Chester. It's your turn to bid. You see, I opened with two diamonds, and Jack passed, and now it's your turn," explained Harry.

"Seven. And we'll make it no trump!" announced Chester suddenly.

The rangers exchanged glances. Harry tried to explain the bidding rules once again. Chester patiently heard him out.

He then proceeded to play out the slam to perfection, and dazzled the rangers with his championship-style play for the rest of the night.

Harry, his partner, remarked: "I tell ya Chester. It's true that it takes you some time to catch on to things. But once you get it, fella, I tell ya. You sure 'nough do get it good!" Turning to the other rangers he crowed, "Man, he's playin', ain't he now?"

That was the night he began to remember. The process of recollection followed a clear pattern. A vague sensation or impression would casually come to him. He had little control over that part. The feelings would just come. The trick was to hold on to the sensation, to savor it. Soon chunks of memory would appear like giant snowflakes and assemble themselves before his eyes, replete with names, dates, and details. Entire events from his past would tumble down to him. For the past few weeks he had become absorbed in this task of remembering and putting things together. He spent much of his time sitting on "his" log in the woods, smoking his pipe, recalling things about his childhood, his parents, his friends. Rapidly he compiled a chronology: his personal history, or autobiography. He had bought a spiral notebook and pencils in Visalia and had begun to write - scribbling on hotel stationery and cafeteria napkins during the day, and then carefully copying and editing his notes during the night. Putting it all down, putting all of his life in order. He called his book Memories. Thus he was writing, or rewriting, the story of his life. The Memories notebook had become an obsession this past week or two. Even now, as he sat over his coffee, he reached down to his backpack and pulled out paper and pencil. He had remembered a trip to Europe he had taken in the seventies, before he had met Marsha.

He looked up. The young woman was still watching him. Her gaze was extremely unsettling. He quickly jotted down some key words: "Sweden, the rain, the hostel by the river, the ride to the museum on the red bus, the rain mostly". Without looking again at the woman across the room, he hurriedly gathered his things, threw on his backpack, and headed out.

The woman had moved faster, though, and met him at the door. She leaned against the door jamb, blocking his exit, her eyes full of anger and determination.

"Excuse me," muttered Chester

"Yah, just like that to excuse you. That's a good one. You're very good!"

"Excuse me?"

"Excuse me! Excuse me!" her voice rising.

Chester stood in the doorway and looked at this woman. He did not know what to do. He decided to put on his gloves. The woman was crying profusely. Tears rolled down her cheeks, curled along her chin, and plopped audibly on the black, rubber floor mat. Her hands were clenched in little fists at her sides, her lower lip trembled. The cashier and the two sisters who worked the souvenir shop had ambled over to the doorway to obtain a better view. Chester observed them from the corner of his eye. He said:

"Come. Let's go, let's talk about it outside."

He reached over her shoulder and pushed on the big heavy door. They stepped out together onto the wet gravel of the parking lot. Her tear-filled eyes remained fixed on him. Finally she blurted out:

"And I thought you were dead! I thought you were dead! You were dead! How did you do it, you thief that is stinking? How do you get away with it? And it's not just the money. It's not just the money!" she cried. "It's me too! How could you do this to me?"

"Do what? What did I do?"

"What you did, you motherfucker," she muttered under her breath.

"We were going to share it,'" she continued mockingly. "We were going to share everything. 'Our whole lives', you said. We were going to share our whole lives. Sharing. And 'together'. That was your word that you liked to say," she smiled sardonically. "But you didn't share anything, did you? You just took the money and you ran, like they say. The minute you had it, you ran. You leave me there to cry..... Thinking that you were dead, you cruel bastard. And my grieving. My grieving! And my heart. You took everything from me......" She began to cry.

"I'm sorry," started Chester in a low voice, "I'm sorry. But I don't remember you..."

"Hah!.... Hah!" she shouted into the cold morning air, her breath condensing in puffs of smoke. That is a good one, Tony. That is a good one."

"Tony?" he queried, his eyes opening wide.

"Ach! That is good. You forget your name too! How do they say it? Yes. A piece of work. Yes, that is it. You are a piece of work, Tony. A piece of work."

"Tony, eh?"

"Yes," with a sarcastic smile, flashing her straight, white teeth.

Chester turned from her and looked up the road. The embankment, the slopes and the long hillsides were covered with glistening snow. The tall pines stood incongruously straight and majestic against the azure sky, as if mocking his feeling of helplessness. He felt a sympathy for this girl, and he felt sorry for himself as well. He needed to understand things, to start from the beginning, to make sense out of this mess. But he couldn't. There was no time. The empty road beckoned to him. The world up the road, the forest that reached up the hillsides, was comprehensible and friendly to him. He wished he could just leave this woman behind, but it wasn't going to be that easy. He looked into the sky, which was clear of clouds, the sun glittering above the treetops.

"So you say that my name is Tony?" he said, squinting into the sun.

She didn't answer.

"Well, maybe it is. Maybe I am Tony," he offered.

His eyes now focused on the tops of the trees, which shifted in the sunlight as a soft breeze moved down from the hilltop.

"Tell me," he said slowly, "is it Tony that I look like?"

Her moist green eyes opened wide, her lips formed a little 'o'. She continued to look at him. She took a step back. She was glaring now. She felt furious at him for introducing this confusion and doubt. For playing the fool, for playing with her as if she were a child. Wasn't it bad enough what he had already done? Her whole body was forged in anger, her fists squeezed tightly at her sides. She noticed, though, that she was able to think very clearly. She had never before been so clear in her life. She was able to restrain herself from striking him. She wanted to strike him, to pummel him. But she knew that she needed to wait. She needed to be patient, to think rationally. She would get her chance. Later. There was still the money, and she knew she mustn't cause a scene. Everyone inside the restaurant was already looking through the windows at them.

"Yes, Tony. You are you. And I am me.... Now, listen carefully to me. You are to walk with me back to the hotel lobby, where I left my suitcase. And then we will take a little walk..... And then maybe you will remember everything. Like where the money is. And like where your head is. And like where the money is again...... Come, Tony. Let us begin to go."

They walked silently along the road over to the hotel. The young woman - he still didn't know her name - efficiently received her suitcase from the reception clerk. She insisted she carry it herself. She scowled at him when he offered to help. They walked up to his little cabin, which was only a few hundred feet further along the road. When he opened the door to the room she entered and loudly dropped the suitcase inside the doorway.

In three noisy, deliberate strides she crossed the little room and ceremoniously sat on the edge of the bed. She opened her purse and busied herself with the lighting of a Marlboro Gold Long. She held out the flame of a wooden match in front of her face and played the tip of the cigarette above the flame until it had lit. Very slowly she exhaled the first drag, the bluish smoke billowing up to the ceiling. She leaned back on the bed and announced:

"That is right, Tony. I have decided to stay. I am staying until you give me the money."

"The name is Chester," he offered lamely.

"OK, Chester. Let it be Chester. What difference does the truth make to a liar? Just give me my share of the money."

"How much is that, your share?"

"$30,000."

"$30,000? Well....That's no problem. I can give you the money. I have it anyway."

"What?.....Where?"

"Right here. In my backpack. And Chester reached over to pull a creased manila envelope out of one of the side pockets. He counted out thirty thousand dollar bills, and handed them to her with a chivalrous bow of his head.

She counted the money, ordered the bills in a neat stack, then placed it officiously in her pocketbook. She eyed Chester suspiciously.

You know, maybe you really aren't Tony."

"Well, I'm glad you....."

"Yah. Tony would never hand money over so easily."

"Yeah. Well, I guess I must be me after all.....What's your name?"

"Andrea. But everybody calls me Andy, right?"

"Andy?"

"Yeah."

"Well, Andy. All I know is that you're a very determined woman. You told off your friends back there in the cafeteria. You seem to know what you want..... Well, I guess money is a simple thing to want..... But all the same, you seem to be very clear and coherent. I can appreciate that, because with me it's just the opposite. I don't know anything anymore, so I can't begin to decide what I want or where I want to go. With me it's a peculiar situation. I know it's hard to believe. I can't believe it myself.......Wait. Let me talk. I can't blame you if you don't believe me.....It's a kind of amnesia I have, a blackout of sorts......

I can tell you, though. I am not your Tony. All the same, even with all my forgetting, I also know that my real problem is not just one of remembering. Eventually I will remember everything. I'm sure of that now and I'm not worried about that anymore. Not much anyway.... I'm just waiting.... Excuse me. Please, excuse me. Excuse me, Andrea, I'm talking too much.....You see, I haven't had the opportunity to talk to anyone openly. But since you already know who I look like, and since now you know who I really am, well then Andrea....Yes, I like Andrea much better than Andy....Anyhow Andrea, I don't often have the chance to talk to anyone. Talking is another thing I seem to have forgotten."

Andrea raised her green eyes to look at Chester. She was angry at herself again, for she realized that she actually felt a sort of pity for this man. She had been listening to his talk and she had actually been believing him. Could it be that this man was not Tony? How could that be? She felt that, in some way, this man was telling the truth, or at least what he thought was the truth. However wild his story sounded, he seemed a sincere person - which Tony was not. But how had this Chester person come to be involved with Tony? Perhaps he was Tony's twin brother? Then again, maybe he really was Tony, her old boyfriend. Maybe he was fooling her again. If so, he was a different Tony. If he was Tony, he had definitely changed. This man did not act like Tony. And if Tony had all that money, he would be in Las Vegas, not in some smelly little cabin. How could all this be? After all, she had attended Tony's "funeral at sea", which she had paid for. And she had received a death certificate. Which she had also paid for.

Andrea slowly put out her cigarette in the plain glass ashtray supplied by the lodge, and rose to examine this Tony, this Chester, this man, in the eyes. To look into someone's eyes is to see through to their soul, so they say.

She stood opposite him, and he stopped talking and returned her gaze. They were Tony's grey-blue eyes, but they had changed somehow. They were more beautiful. They were moist, open eyes. When she tried to look into them, through them, past them, when she tried to look into his soul, she felt a jolt, a pull, an enormous sympathy. She and this man were one thing, tied together, different parts of the same soul. She felt drawn to him, and she stepped closer.

She had thought of a test.

"Tony, give me a kiss."

"A kiss?" Chester started.

'Yeah, kiss me. Come on. I want it."

"No..... er, I'm not really allowed to..." Chester mumbled.

Andrea moved forward and began to kiss Chester on the lips. Not just once but repeatedly, pressing her lips on his, then licking his lips gently with her tongue. He began to feel the pleasure of her, and the pleasure of being aroused. He had forgotten......

Suddenly she stopped and looked into his eyes again. She examined his eyes patiently. They were more grey than blue; they were anguished and very deep; they were beautiful, moist and innocent eyes; they were definitely not Tony's eyes. She touched his cheek softly with the back of her hand, as he gazed at her incredulously.

"No," she whispered, as she caressed his eyes with her own, "you are not Tony."

"No. I'm not," he pleaded, "I'm Chester. Chester Knowles..... or at least I used to be..... But I look like this Tony fellow, don't I? ....It's very strange, Andrea......You see, I was dying. I remember that clearly..... I was dying. I was a goner. And then I wanted to be alive. That's the main thing I remember. I wanted to be alive."

Chester turned away from her and began to pace noisily back and forth in the little room, his steps resounding on the wooden floor.

"Actually," he continued excitedly, "the main thing, the main thing that I remember, was a feeling. A very strong feeling. The main thing was that I didn't want to die like that, on the floor, without any dignity, like some dog or something."

"So, you stayed alive."

"But my face! My face! And my body, too...... I don't know why they're different!" he exclaimed, as he walked to the other side of the little room.

"I guess my desire," he continued, "my desire to live, wound me up with a different face.... Tony's face, right?" He stopped to look her straight in the eyes. She nodded her head slowly in assent.

"And I've also acquired his money, right? And it's your money too, you say.... And, oh, that's OK.... Let me tell you, I don't even want to know how you came by all that money. Believe me, Andrea, I don't want any of this."

"I just want to go home.......And I know now where my home is. I know where it is. And where they are.....I know that ..... but...."

He paused, his voice choking. Looking down at the wood floor, he felt tears filling his eyes.

"Say, Tony.... Say, Mr. Chester," she said, delicately placing her hand around his neck, "don't be so difficult on yourself. It's not so bad, you're still alive after all."

"You're very nice, Andrea," he muttered, looking into her eyes again.

Slowly their faces drew nearer. And then they kissed long and deeply.

"Say, Chester. What do you think would happen if we made love?"

"Here? You mean here? Well, I don't know," muttered Chester, sheepishly looking down at the cabin floor.

"Say, Chester," she smiled softly, "give me a kiss. Come on. Come on now."

She peeled off her ski jacket with her free hand, and pressed herself against him.

A Previous Body

Tony Marcos, rock and roll drummer and part-time drug dealer, dreamed that he had died and gone to heaven. Unaccountably, there was lots of money in his pockets: billfolds jammed-full of all kinds of big-denomination bills. Thousands of dollars in his pockets! Also in Tony's heaven was a stock portfolio set up over the phone, managed by a New York financial advisor, who had put him into mostly speculative issues, as well as some high-interest municipal bonds and preferred stocks. Tony held bank accounts in several cities. He had keys to several safety deposit vaults. There was an ounce each of coke and grass in the glove compartment of his van - which was now fixed and running like a top. Tony was a rich man. He was gliding along. He was walking tall.

A beautiful woman walked on either side of him. There was a rhythm - the whole dream had a rhythm - of a vintage Wilson Pickett recording. Down to the horns. Tony sported a freshly-pressed, dark blue suit, as he strode down the street. His tie was silk. His shoes were the very best alligator skins, and were mysteriously silent on the sidewalk. His white hair flowed in the soft summer breeze as he strolled up Chicago's State Street - the blond on one arm, the Afro chick on the other. People eyed him admiringly, respectfully. They recognized him because he was a big star. A big rock and roll star. With an album in the top ten. He was walking tall. Real tall.

Chicago now stretched out before him like an aerial map. He could see Lake Michigan shining in the morning sun. He felt himself rising up higher and higher. He could now peer down at the flat plains of the Midwest as if from a hot-air balloon. "Hey," he said to himself, "I'm flying." The Rocky Mountains loomed up on him, and then the blue of the Pacific. "Oh, oh. I'm about to leave the atmosphere. I need a little more atmosphere. Should have taken some with me. Hey, I think I need some atmosphere."

Tony opened his eyes and breathed in deeply. Bands of yellow light sliced through the vertical blinds, and stretched diagonally across the wall-to-wall carpet. The light beams buzzed with energy. Its buzzing was something alive. He had arrived at another place. Where was he? Was this another dream? No, it was not another dream. It was real. He was in Andy's bed. Andy, his girlfriend. He was in her bed, and she had already left for work. He turned over in the bed. His shoes were on the floor by his bedside; he could smell them. They were his old, familiar, worn-out shoes. And they lay on their sides on the fuzzy carpet like dead fish. Some heaven, he thought, I'm still back where I was. If life were a board game, I would be still on square one. Glued to square one, square zero even.

He pulled himself over and squatted on the edge of the sagging Futon bed. The Los Angeles morning already suggested a day of heat. Andy had left for work - a waitressing job at a cafe down the block. Tony had a fuzzy recollection that she had spoken to him earlier this morning just before she left. She had said something, something important. What was it? Dammit, he couldn't remember. Well, maybe if I don't think about it, he told himself, then I'll remember it. That's what they say. He had heard this piece of advice on a videotape titled *Improve Your Mind*. It said that if you want to remember something then it was best to not try to remember anything at all. But what they didn't mention on that damned videotape, he mused, is that as soon as you try not to think of something, that's exactly when you can't stop trying to think of it. And then your brain starts working overtime, and everything starts pouring into your head, and then it starts swirling around, and then you can just forget about it altogether.......... OK, he told himself. Let's just calm down. He breathed deeply, counting to five on each inhalation.

He had woken up late; he had been stoned the night before. He had slept with Andy, but they hadn't had sex. He had dreamed a wonderful dream, but he could not remember what it was. He had been flying, but lacked atmosphere. That's all he could remember. Tony extended his arms in front of him and checked his hands to see if they trembled. They were OK. He thought to himself, "Dammit! What's the difference? I'm not playing drums anyway. And if I don't play the drums, what the hell does it matter about my hands? And what does anything matter anyway? And what the hell am I supposed to do today? I don't even know what it is I want. Oh, man! But what was it that Andy told me?"

Tony combed his bony fingers through his white hair. Six months ago he had arrived in Los Angeles with his long-in-the-tooth dream of becoming a rock and roll star. It was to be his last and final dream. He would soon be dead. He was already 38 years old, too old for the rock and roll thing, anyway. The sixties were over. So were the seventies and the eighties. The dream was gone. Aah, but not for Tony. He was still dreaming. Apparently no one had informed Tony Marcos about the nineties, not to mention the third millennium, which was fast approaching. Tony still lived the dream. His father, a bricklayer from Palermo who had come to Detroit via Brooklyn, insisted that Tony's brains had gotten messed up from watching too much television. "His brains, they caput. It's the damn television, I swear it."

Tony's father was just getting started, as the family sat down at their places around the oblong table and solemnly faced their plates of spaghetti and meatballs.

"It's that damn television what makes his brains stupid. I swear it. The television, it makes him want all kinda things that he cainta' have. Things that ain't hisself."

When Tony was eight years old his Aunt Anna had taken him to the old Palace Theater on Market Street in Detroit to see Walt Disney's Pinocchio. The little wooden puppet, who was Italian, but "not a Sicilian", as Aunt Anna informed him, made wishes which later came true. The trick was to be good and to wish very strongly and intently. "When you wish upon a star your dreams come true" - it remained Tony's favorite song. What a great disillusionment to learn in later adulthood that dreams don't really come true. Never. They never came true. It was all a lot of crap. Nevertheless, whenever Tony would chance to see a solitary star at night, he would make a wish. When he spilled salt, he would throw some over his shoulder. When he saw a ladder he walked around it.

Conversely, he had become a bit of a philosopher. He pondered, albeit cynically and sarcastically, about the "meaning of life". He had become marginally involved in the Scientology movement, and was a firm believer in the "power of positive thinking". He had the seven-video collection called The Power of the Mind, which featured animated demonstrations of astral bodies and psychokinetic phenomena. The mind was a powerful thing. It was capable of anything. Tony was sure of it. Therefore, it was important to be hopeful and to have good thoughts. It might even help to pray. And secretly Tony prayed. He prayed more than anything else that he could succeed: "Oh God. If only people could listen to my music!"

His dream was to live a life of good music, a life of realization, a life of artistic creation and true freedom. To stretch it out, the dream was to live on a sort of perpetual high, a smooth and easy high. The goal was to live a life that was worth living, a life that felt like a good rock and roll chord progression, a life that had the feel of a good rhythm and blues song, with a good hard beat. A life to sing to, to dance to.....

It was definitely a musical type of dream.

Unfortunately, as Tony eventually discovered, dreams and reality are separated by a wide gulf. In actuality, a chasm. Reality in the music biz meant a collection of markets, each very specialized. Each market was like a citadel, practically impenetrable. It was a matter of who you knew rather than what you knew, just like they say. It was nearly impossible to get your foot in the door. It was all a matter of marketing, they told him. Marketing shmarketing, Tony didn't want to hear about it any more. He just knew that his music was good, and that people didn't want to hear good music anymore. It wasn't his fault that no one was interested in his music. Never mind that it was great rock n' roll: Beatles, Stones, Tempts, all the Motown stuff, Creedence Clearwater Revival. All good stuff. Class material. Why was it that no one wanted to listen? What had gone wrong with the world?

Tony had gotten as lost as a solitary star in the vastness of the evening sky. He was out there by himself. The music was no longer any fun; there was no living in it. His prime source of income these days came from the peddling of drugs, mostly cocaine. And even at drug peddling, he was a decided failure. Nobody wanted to buy from him, deal with him. The dream ended for him here in LA. The continent ended here. There were no more chances.

Tony looked around at the small apartment. Andy's apartment. Good thing he had met Andy. Otherwise he'd be sleeping out on the street, or in one of the alleyways off

Third Street. His car - his traveling van, his wheels, his Silver Bullet - was at the garage collecting dust. His drums were in hock someplace on Sunset Blvd. His plan of putting together another band was already in shambles.

Tony used to go by the name Silver Bullet, for his hair was prematurely gray - actually it was white as snow. Silver Bullet had been his name since the old days in Detroit. The name and the long white hair had been his trademark - an asset for him, particularly in Vegas, where it helped to look "respectable" and "mature". But as his luck would have it, in the 80's, Bob Seger had stolen the name for his band. And then Coors Beer used the name in their commercials! Everyone was using his name! So now, in the middle of sets, people would call out to him "Hey buddy! How 'bout a beer?" His stage name, his asset, had become an embarrassment, a joke. He tried to sue, but that was a wash. What did he get for it? Nothing, not a penny, not a dime. His lawyer back in Chicago had told him not to worry, he was still working on it. Bull crap!

So his stage name had been hijacked. The rug had been pulled out from under his feet. His drums were torn and in hock. His amps were in storage. His van, his traveling van with the words The Lone Ranger and the Silver Bullets emblazoned on the side panels, was out of commission and needed a valve job, probably a new engine. It was in the shop of some thief of a mechanic down on La Cienega Blvd.

So he was stuck in LA. At the end of the continent. He was like a ghost, a dead man. The kids on Sunset Blvd eyed him suspiciously. The women in Beverly Hills didn't even notice him when he walked by. The young creeps who now ran the studios didn't know who he was anymore. He was an old man in a young business. Even in Vegas, he was too old. He hated to play Vegas anyway. People didn't listen to you there. It was just background music.

So he had left Vegas and driven to Palm Springs, where he sold $30,000 worth of coke. Then he had come to LA to put together a new group. What he wound up with was a group of young punks, worthless punks - only one of whom could actually play guitar. All that was left in the business nowadays were these skinny little punks. Tony had spent a good chunk of his cash on studio time. He had needed to teach them everything, the Bozos. And even they had left him the week before to go back to Vegas. Good! Let them try their luck in Vegas with their big connection. Some connection, a big fat guy who dealt cocaine, a god-dammed bartender! Davy was a nice guy, but he was definitely not a serious connection.

He sat on the edge of the bed and looked at his shoes that lay on the carpet: pointy, grey, alligator skins. Old shoes. Tony grimaced. They had looked so great when he had bought them back in Detroit. He had worn them on stage for seven years. He had polished them regularly, but now there was no denying that they were finished, kaput - frayed on the stitching and too scuffed up to wear on stage anymore. Maybe he could sell them. People in L.A. liked to buy these kinds of things: things that were supposedly cool, things that they thought were cool, things that they thought other people would think was cool. He had even seen several stores down on Beverly Blvd that actually specialized in used cowboy boots.

It was an unbelievable city. Everything was image, and image could be recycled, sold again. He reached down for his boots and then flung them against the wall. He had come out here hoping to make more than just a couple of bucks on his boots. He had wanted to hit it big. He had wanted to succeed. Have people listen to his music. Do the American dream if he couldn't do his own dream. He pulled himself up to his feet. Too many dreams. And too much hangover from too much cocaine the night before.

He remembered the cocaine, and rushed to the drawer to see if it was still there. Oh my God, it wasn't there. Where was it? Where the hell?..... Ah, there it is sitting innocently in its plastic baggie on the coffee table. Like a silent, white creature. Just waiting for him. Carefully, Tony lifted the bag by the edge. Efficiently he prepared a quick hit, licking his fingers when he was done, playing it around his gums. It was enough. It was good stuff, just right. This was the stuff he was going to sell...Well, he had already used quite a bit of it for himself, and he still needed to go back to Vegas, or maybe Barstow, to get some more. But never mind, he'd get it if it was the last thing he did. And then he remembered! That was what Andy had spoken about this morning before she left! It was all perfectly clear now.

Andy had stood alongside the bed. Her thigh was alongside his face. Her thigh was such a thing of beauty, so smooth. She rustled and jostled him with her arm.

"Tony, oof Tony," she was pleading,

"Yes that is right, you sleepy one. Wake up. That is right, wake up... Now you are listening?" Tony lifted his head off the pillow.

"Good. Now listen: Tony, I will be seeing with you this morning at ten o'clock at the restaurant. And Carlos will also be there and then you two will talk over a cup of coffee, as they say. And you will make what it is you want to do. For yourself, and for me, too. So do not forget."

And then she had pivoted, and he had watched her long, sleek, tan legs amble across the room toward the door. And then the beautiful legs had come back toward him, and she had leaned over, her short waitress skirt rising, as she kissed him on the cheek.

"Ciao, mi carison."

So Tony remembered. He had remembered it all with no effort. For sure it was the coke. It had made him forget, and then it had made him remember. Andy had set up this meeting for him. A big move. Ah Andy! Beautiful young Andy. Andy from Amsterdam. Andy was going to save him. The girl was going to make him money - to the tune of 60,000 buckaroos. He had told her that they would get out of LA, that they would make a new start. He would take her with him. And he meant it this time. It was his last chance, the end of the continent and all.

As he walked toward the Bagel Place, he continued to think of Andy. He pictured her green eyes, her little nose, her dirty blond hair, her smile. There was a sweetness about her, a simplicity, a sincerity. And yet she was very intelligent. Usually intelligence messes a person up, makes them too talkative, too nervous. Intelligent people were usually a pain in the ass. But not Andy. Andy was just right. Andy was like a dream. Andy was even better than a dream. She was real.

She would be there at the restaurant for him. Working, poor thing. Her weekday shift started at six. How did she ever get up so early? Three months he had been living with her, and she always woke up early, made it to work on time. She was never late. She was a dependable person. And she took care of him. Supported him. She was keeping him going until he got another band going. Andy had loved his music right away. More than anything else, that was why he loved her. She knew music. She listened. Even though she was from Holland, she knew American music thoroughly, and she had good taste. She liked the oldies.

Tony looked at his gold wristwatch as he walked up Third Street. It was ten-thirty already. Never mind, Andy will still be there, and this Carlos will still be there too. Let the bastard wait. Tony smiled his first smile of the day.

It was with a Colombian guy, and it was always tricky when you dealt with Colombians. You never knew where you stood. This guy Carlos was quite a piece of work. He didn't look like much, but he had big-time backing, or so he claimed, and he had the cash to pay for any kind of dope - or so he claimed. Andy knew Carlos from the restaurant. Or so she claimed. Tony suspected that she knew him from before. But that was none of his business. Really, it was none of his business. It was in the past she had said. The main thing was that Andy had offered to set up the deal. Andy liked a snort here and there, just like any other chick. But she was not a user, simply wasn't into it.

She was doing this whole deal for him. Just for him. And he had told her that he would split the money fifty-fifty. And he had meant it, too. So, she was a business partner. But Andy was more than that. Andy was different. She really cared. She was a sincere person. She was from Holland, she was beautiful. She was gentle, educated, cultured. And she loved him. That's what made everything different. She loved him. And he, Tony Marcos, was actually coming to love her too. More than he had loved anyone before. More than his ex-wife Carolyn, more than Susan, his woman in Chicago, more than anyone.

The stores on Third Street were nice and laid-back this morning. The people on the sidewalk floated by in a pleasant haze. This L.A. world had a rhythm: a minor key seventh chord alternating with a sixth. A mellow beat, a pleasant hum from the dope.

Andy was not in the restaurant when he stepped in. He sat down at a small corner table near the door. He looked around for Carlos. Where was he? And where was Andy, anyway? She must be in the back. He drummed his fingers on the small wooden table. Andy wasn't coming. Perhaps she wasn't there at all. Maybe she had canceled the deal. Could he trust her? He grated his wooden chair noisily, as he got up from his table and strode toward the kitchen. Just as he approached the swinging doors, Andy stepped out. They almost collided.

"Jeez Andy," he smiled, as he placed his hand gently on her hip.

"Oof, Tony. You are too impossible."

"Sorry Andy, I'm sorry..."

"Listen to me, Tony," she whispered with urgency, "Carlos is here. There - at the table by the window." She motioned with her head. "Come." She walked him over to a young, chubby kid, with a two-day growth of beard over acne pimples, who eyed them playfully from the rim of his cappuccino.

"So, Carlos. It's good to see you again." Tony extended his hand.

"Yes. Good for you. Maybe good for me too." Carlos reached up for Tony's hand, and squeezed it with surprising strength.

Carlos wasted no time, and the deal was soon set: $60,000. Tony needed to drive back to Barstow for the pick-up. That his van was in the shop, that he wasn't certain of his contact in the desert, and that he only had three days to get it all done....well, that would all take care of itself.

"Don't worry, Carlos. We'll have everything done by Thursday night. And it's really good stuff. Let me tell you man...."

"Tell me shit. You just have the stuff. And I will have the money. And that's it. Finito. And why should you be talk so much?"

"Ain't he absolutely the absolute, my man Tummie?" said Carlos, turning expansively toward a bulky young man in baggy jeans and tee shirt, who had slipped in the door, and now had sidled alongside the table.

"Absolutely the absolute. Like the vodka. Abso. Abso."

"OK, man." he said, turning to Tony, "That's it. I see you Thursday night. Pero late. Like around three? AM, right? Like after everythin's closed? You get it?"

Carlos flipped a crisp, folded, fifty dollar bill on the table. It landed on its edge and rested on the table like a butterfly.

"Hey! OK, my man. See you...." Tony called. But Carlos and Tummie were already gone. The door closed with a click.

Andy and Tony

"I tell ya, we're gonna be all right, Andy," called Tony from the shower.

"What?" she shouted back.

"I mean, you won't have to work at that Bagel Place any more. And you, I mean we, ... can do what we want."

"But I like the Bagel Place," answered Andy from the hallway. She was drying her long hair. She had one large pink towel wrapped around her body, and she used another towel to dry her hair.

"OK, so you can buy your own Bagel Place! " he yelled as he shut off the shower. "I mean, we can buy our own....Well, maybe not a bagel place. Maybe somethin' more like a pizza store, or maybe...Well, I don't know exactly what kind of place exactly.... whatever we want. That's the point."

"OK, Tony. Stop to getting your mind into a confused state. The main point is whatever we want."

"Yeah. And together, Andy. Together! Me and you, all the way together," crooned Tony, as he emerged from the bathroom and reached to embrace her.

"Oof, Tony. Go away!" she squawked, as she moved to elude his grasp. "And to put on some clothes would be a proper thing to do. This is Los Angeles, not Chicago." She walked into the bedroom, threw the towels on the bed, and started to dress.

Later, as they walked over to the Beverly Center, Tony resumed his pitch.

"You know, we're in this together, Andy."

"Yes, my love."

"Tomorrow, I go get the van with the money we get now from Rebecca. You're sure she's still at the store? Yeah? OK, then. I mean, as soon as we make the money, we pay her right back, so no sweat there. Right, Andy?"

"Right, Tony. But only to stop talking so much about it!"

"I know. I can't help it. It's just that things are finally starting to look up."

Andrea didn't answer, but smiled quietly to herself. Tony was happy. Maybe Tony would be lucky, too. Luck is better than brains, so they said. She felt good for Tony. Perhaps they would have a future together. Perhaps.

Andrea looked around at the traffic on Third Street. It was nearly eight o'clock, and the streets were full. The heat of the day, the warm air of the city, and now the wonderful shift toward nighttime: all spoke in a great harmonious hum. Los Angeles was a wonderful city. Everywhere the world was wonderful, a reflection of the glory of our Lord. Perhaps Tony was a bit out of step, a bit silly. But never mind. He was happy, and so was she. She gripped his hand tightly. She closed her eyes as she walked, trusting in Tony. Yes, she could trust him.

Andrea and Chester

Andrea Van Khymer found herself the next morning lying alongside the quietly sleeping body of Chester Knowles. With each breath his body rose and fell like a ship on a soft, calm sea. Andrea lay silently on her back, her hands folded behind her head, and considered her predicament. She was definitely in a predicament.

Definitely, very definitely, this man lying next to her was not her Tony. Tony had made love entirely differently. This man, this Chester, kissed differently, he did the sex differently, he felt differently inside. This man Chester - she loved his name - did everything in a very beautiful way. He was like an artist. He was present in the lovemaking, and also he was a thousand miles away. There was something abstract about him, and yet he also was very passionate. Whoever had said that all men were alike was just crazy. Maybe they all wanted the same thing, sex. Maybe they all saw women in the same way...Well, not even that part was true.

Each man saw women differently. In a different way, his own way. It was like a feature of their personality. Their perception of women was what defined them, really. So men were all different. Very different. And this Chester was different from Tony. That was the primary fact here. Men were all different, in their lovemaking, that is, and by their lovemaking they were defined, really they were, and this Chester was totally different from Tony in his lovemaking. Entirely different.

Then she asked herself why it was that God had played this trick on her. And why must it always be God?

Well, if it wasn't God, then who was it that was playing these tricks on her? The devil? She rolled over on her side to look at Chester's head on the pillow next to her: his clean, white hair, his child-like, innocent face - yes, his face was actually a bit different from Tony's. It was a more angular kind of face; she liked his face. She could love this man, too. The day before she had made love to him because she had been at a loss. It had just come to her. Her father used to joke when they played cards: "when in doubt, throw an ace". So she did. And, well, also, she had wanted to do it for some reason.

It had felt right, and there was no doubt about it. It had been all right. But, still, it had been a silly thing to do. Because, now as she gazed on him sleeping so sweetly on the pillow, she knew that she had fallen in love with him. It was definitely a problem it was - the way she fell in love all the time. She smiled. Her friend Sally had called it an addiction, this falling-in-love problem. There were therapeutic groups for such addictions, said Sally. In America they had therapeutic groups for everything, of course. Therapy was another business. That's how America was. Still, as she leaned on her elbow and examined her latest "problem", Andrea knew that this time it was something special. It was different this time. God had placed a miracle in front of her. She placed her hand on her little breast. Her heart was beating so strongly and steadily. She smiled and remembered a prayer from her childhood: "God please, show me Thy mercy. Show Thy mercy to me. And let Thy will be done. I am ready God. I am ready." She made the sign of the cross across her chest.

The sunlight poured through the little window, through the lacy, white curtain, warming Andrea's feet and legs as she lay motionless under the sheet and blanket. She moved to curl her body up against Chester's and she slept again. She dreamt about her father. He was looking at her, talking to her. But he wasn't really talking. He wasn't speaking words. He was talking to her without words. He was telling her that "It was all right. All is well now." The light slowly edged up her sleeping body while she slept - until it cast its brightness upon her face. She squinted into the white brightness, letting her lashes play with the incoming light to create fluttering, spectral patterns.

"Are you ready?" came a deep voice from a place inside of her. Was she still dreaming?

She turned to look at Chester. He was sitting on the edge of the bed, smiling a wide, wonderful, boyish grin. He looked so happy, looking at her over his shoulder. She spun her body toward him, wrapped her long arms tight around his bare chest to pull herself close. She kissed him deeply on the neck. She wanted to kiss him all over. To never stop.

"Hey, hey," he chuckled, "C'mon. I'm not such a young man anymore. I'm an old guy with this white hair! Actually, who the heck knows how old I am? C'mon let's get ready. We gotta go."

"Where? Where do we have to go, my love?"

"Breakfast! First things first. Breakfast, my love. I may not know who I am, or how I got here, but I do know that man must eat. And so must woman. And the cafeteria's open only till nine. And then it is closed till 11:30. Closed! So the latecomers wind up buying Chips Ahoy cookies and Mr. Salty pretzels at the general store. That's what you wind up with for breakfast if you're late - along with hot chocolate from the machine, and it's terrible hot chocolate. And it's not even hot. Believe me, I've been here all winter. If you don't make it there on time for the breakfast........"

"Chips Ahoy are good. I like Chips Ahoy," murmured Andrea as she ran her tongue along his arm and up to his neck. "Ooh, and you are salty too. I think I have my Mr. Salty here in this bed!"

Tony Approaches his Death

"I'm tsorry, my frient. I can't do nothsing about dat."

"Yes, but...... But listen..... I mean I gotta have a car. And it doesn't necessarily have to be the van. I understand now about the van..."

"Dat's right my friend. The van still needs to be put in the gasket, and den we need to...."

"OK, OK," exclaimed Tony, waving some fifty dollar bills in the air, "not for the van. You keep the van... for now at least. Listen. All I need is a car for today. I'll have it back tonight. Tonight. And you can hold this hundred and fifty dollars. Plus the van as collateral. I'll sign whatever you want."

The wrinkled, sun-dried face of the mechanic softened as he stepped toward Tony. He brought his wrench up to Tony's chest, his face inches from Tony's, and looked intently into Tony's eyes for a long moment.

"OK," he agreed at last with an easy smile, nodding with the wrench again, "OK."

"Miguel! Miguel!" he barked, turning toward the garage. Big Miguel ambled over, wiping his hands on a dirty towel. "Miguel, go get this gentleman the red Toyota."

"It's a goot car," he declared, as he turned again to Tony. "My son's been driving it till last week. And I just put in it a new water pump. Dat's all. It runs like a fucking Porsche. You just have it back before tonight."

He plucked the cash from Tony's hand and stuffed it into the pants pocket of his grimy overalls.

And that was that. Tony headed down La Cienega to the Number 10, the San Bernardino freeway. He had a meeting set with Davey, the bartender from Vegas who had the dope. He met Davey at 2 PM, at their appointed meeting place, a Carl's Juniors in Indio. Davey was busy eating; he had spread a newspaper over the formica table like a tablecloth. Davey raised his head and nodded to Tony. He finished his mouthful, and wiped his mouth with one of the paper napkins he had piled on the newspaper.

"Hope you don't mind. I started eatin' without 'cha. I tell ya, these Big Star things are the best. You know people go to McDonald's and to the Burger Kings, and the whatnots, but lemme tell you, Carl's is the best....... I heard he was a fascist, though...... Never mind, they all are. If you're gonna boycott all the fascists, then you probably wind up starvin' ta death. And what kinda car are you're gonna drive? They're all fascists. Aaah. Sit down, Tony. Sit down. Don't just stand there. And don't worry, I brought those tickets to the ball game like I promised ya. Ya sure ya don't want nothin' ta eat?"

Davey was an enormous old guy, maybe three hundred pounds.

"OK, Davey. I'll have a burger too."

"Get the Big Star. They're the best."

Tony soon returned with his tray, and squeezed in opposite Davey.

"Before we talk any business, Tony, lemme ask you how your singin's been comin'. Are you playing? No? That's a shame. What with a voice like yours… Well, like I told ya, I can find you a nice job at one of the hotels. Anytime, Tony. Because I remember you, Tony. You're a fella with .....how shall I say it?.....Integrity. Towards the music, at least. ... Say, you know those boys you sent me? The guitarists? Jesus, what a bunch! And I'm not talkin' about how they look, neither. I mean how they came to me, and well, they said you had said such and such, which I figured you hadn't said nothin' about. Am I right? Yeah? ......Well, what the hell, I finally got them a job. At a small place. Nothin' much, but for them it's O.K. They got themselves a new drummer. He ain't bad, neither. But, if you wanted to come back...No? Well, that's your choice, Tony."

Davey raised his giant body from the table. His bottom protruded like the transatlantic shelf. He waddled over to the waste basket to dump his wrappers in the receptacle.

"O.K. Tony. Lemme show you those tickets. Ya done eatin'? 'Cause I gotta start headin' back. I'm workin' tonight."

Davey and Tony went out to the parking lot and entered Davey's Cadillac, where he handed Tony the cocaine in a double plastic bag. Tony quickly opened the plastic tie, and dipped his finger into the bag for a taste.

"Ya know, Tony, you like that shit too much. I seen guys roasted and fried, and stuck with a fork in 'em when they was done. All over that powder. Now me, I work the bar. Nearly my whole life I work bars. Have I ever taken a drink? No sir. No. You gotta keep your nose clean, pardon the expression. Hey, that was a good one, keepin' yer nose clean..... O.K. Tony, ya got the money, don'tcha? C'mon, I gotta go."

"Yeah, me too. A long drive back to LA. It's good stuff. Thanks, Davey. I figure this is my last run like this. But maybe I'll be back in Vegas. Anywaze, I'll see ya. Thanks for this deal, Dave."

"Why? Ya think I didn't make somethin' on it? Take it easy Tony. And try 'an get some sense inta ya brains instead of all that powder."

Tony drove back to LA in a troubled state of mind. Davey was right. He looked stupid, but he had common sense, sechel as Davey put it. Yeah, but how to do it? How to live a good life? It wasn't easy. Time was running out, damn it. Tony's thin fingers squeezed the steering wheel of the rented '78 Toyota Corolla. His eyes were set straight ahead on the road, the freeway lane striping's flying under the car - too fast to count, but slow enough to be individually discernible. Why do they have to paint those damned stripes anyway? They don't keep people in their lanes anyway, and they're annoying. Everything, all of life, was rushing by. Why did it have to be so fast? Why did it have no meaning? Why must it be so hard?

It occurred to Tony as he sat driving on the freeway that he might never make sense of it all. There might not never be any light at the end of the tunnel, and no pot of gold at the end of the rainbow. No rainbow period. He had always assumed that at some point he'd put it all together, get all the pieces of the puzzle to fit. He'd been waiting all his life for his dreams to come true. He'd been waiting for success, for recognition, for admiration as a musician. He felt he deserved it. He'd been waiting all this time. Up until this moment it was just a question of when. It was just a matter of controlling his impatience and anger, a matter of maintaining positive thoughts. Eventually he would get it all together. Eventually he would taste success. Eventually he'd be able to understand it all.

But as he watched the road speed by, the thought seized him that life had passed him by already. Life was like one of the road markings. Racing past. Gone in the blink of an eye. Even though he was on his way back to Los Angeles, even though he had the cocaine and was set to make a big score, there was no gladness, no sense of victory. He had overcome a number of obstacles in order to swing this deal. But something was wrong. He felt strange, weird. He had read in one of his books about "floating anxiety". Well, whatever it was, he had it in "floating" spades.

All the same, he had the cocaine in the car - tucked carefully under the passenger seat. Because he had taken a lot of hits from the bag back home, he was a little bit short. A bit less than what he should have had, but maybe he could put it past Carlos as the full $60,000 worth. It was very good stuff, and good stuff, real good stuff, is never easy to come by. He had made it to Palm Springs in this old Corolla the mechanic lent him (not really such a bad guy after all, that mechanic). Everything would seem to be all right. But yet it wasn't. The feeling in his stomach told him otherwise. He felt an actual physical illness. Fear, in the form of chills, ran through his chest and arms. His knuckles bared white on the steering wheel.

What was hardest to swallow was that he was not going to "get it". He was not going to obtain any wisdom. He was not going to get any smarter. If anything, he was more confused than ever. Recently, he had become nearly incapable of thinking any kind of serious thoughts. He had those video tapes about the human mind, but he had no patience to watch them anymore. Perhaps he had grown too cynical. How had that happened? Where had all the time gone? Where was the little boy he used to be? The little boy who looked up at the big screen at the Palace Theatre in Detroit? The teen-aged wonder, who could bang the heck out of the skins? The talented young musician, who was sure to make it? Where were all these people from the past?

He was a middle-aged man already. He was almost thirty-eight years old. Where had his life gone? In the blink of an eye he'd become an old man - a man whose life had just gone by. Several tears fell onto his lap. He was crying! He eased up on the gas pedal. The needle on the speedometer moved from eighty down to a bit under seventy miles an hour. No sense inviting trouble. After all he was carrying.

The sun had finally set. The sky ahead showed a pale orange. The L.A. haze lay low over the city and spread an orange light across the horizon. The grey of the freeway ramps, the nondescript suburban landscape, was bathed in a soft luminescence. Off to the north, on Tony's right as he looked out the side window, was a star, the first star. Tony closed his damp eyes for a moment to squeeze out a final tear, and he made a wish. "Good star, forget about me. Just let Andy come out of this OK."

Andrea

Chester and Andrea sat on the trunk of a fallen redwood. Surrounding them were irregular patches of snow, icy and glistening at the edges. The snow resembled human fingers and hands that reached out and stretched over the steep terrain. Imperceptibly, inexorably, the snow was melting, soaking into the earth, moving into the roots of the trees, and then up into the branches, out into the piney leaves. The big trees loomed tall over them. Andrea spun her head around. She had never seen anything like it. She had seen mountains in Europe, but never in the winter. In Israel, she had seen some mountain snow in Jerusalem and in the Galilee hills. But it was nothing like this. The mountains here were very much grander. They filled the whole world. And it seemed like the two of them, she and Chester, sat in the center of it.

The slope of the mountain beckoned like a friend; behind them, down the long hill, the cottages and cabins of the lodge waited silently.

"Andrea?"

"Yes."

"You know what I want? I want you to tell me about yourself."

"Me?"

"Yes."

"You want the long version or the short version?"

"The long one, of course. Tell me everything."

"OK...OK...Well, it all started many years ago...eighteen years ago....But I was so very little at that time that I do not remember anything."

"No. Really."

"All right then. Twenty-eight years ago that I was born. In Amsterdam, my home city. On Ruysch Straat. Well, actually I was born in the hospital, the municipal hospital, which was sitting only several streets away from our house, actually. Many times, we used to walk past the hospital on our way, and my father would say to me, "That's where you were born, did you know that?" He thought it was a funny thing to say. Anyway, it was three kilos and a half en I was, more than seven of your pounds. They say I was a difficult baby, always wanting to be picked up and coddled......do you really want to hear all of this rot?.... Well, it was a long time ago. You must remember that I was only a baby, you know - that is a joke......It's interesting, I've never done this before....."

"Done what?"

"This!...You know. To tell about yourself. To recount your own history...."

"Yes. I do know. Very well. I've been doing it to myself the past two weeks. Nearly all the time I've been doing it. It is interesting, like you say. So go on. Tell me about yourself as a baby." Chester leaned forward on the log.

"Well actually, I do have only this one singular memory of myself as a baby. Perhaps I was two or three years old. No, I was more littler than that. Because in the memory I am standing up in my bed. What do they call it? A bed with wooden bars...."

"A crib."

"Yes. Holding on to the bars on the sides of the wooden cribs. I remember the sighting of my fists as they held the rails. And I remember standing there such a long time, such a very long time, calling for my oma, my mom.....And she didn't come........"

"No?"

"Noooh, she didn't come. At least that's what I remember. And…. that's it……. I only remember standing there holding the railing. It is such a clear picture. Just waiting for my oma to come. I cannot remember that she came. I only remember the waiting."

Chester looked off into the forest. A lone bird, a whipp-o-will, chirped forth in bold trills from a low branch nearby. The clear noonday sky bespoke a quiet optimism.

"Chester?"

He extended his arm and rested it on her hip. He said: "So, where is your mother now?"

"Oh," she said dreamily, tilting back her head to look at the branches high, high up, "My mother……. Well, she is still in Amsterdam of course. She is very fine. They still live on Ruysch Straat, although they have purchased the apartment next to door, and the house is much bigger now, even though they don't really need so much rooms any longer. My mother is very busy these days, as she has returned to her work after all these years. She is a social worker. She works at a kind of orphanage, a school for boys. We write letters, she writes the most beautiful letters. My father, however, he does not write."

"Why is that?"

"Oh. That is complicated. He hasn't…. Well, he hasn't been able to forgive me for something that happened…. Something that... involved a young man……. When I was 22 years old. I had just finished my studies. Or rather, I had almost to finish them….. Well, you see…… there was this young man. Federico was his name. And well, I loved him very much. And we wanted to marry…..and to move to Barcelona. You see I had met Federico in Barcelona, at the art museum. And then he had followed me to Amsterdam. And we had been together. As a man and a woman. It was the first time for me, the first real time. However, it was a bit difficult. Difficult... because I needed to make a decision. Because for the reason that Federico wanted us to marry.... And I confronted my parents. I asked them. I asked how they felt. About my getting into marriage with Federico. After all, there was a cultural distance. Federico was Catholic, and he was Spanish. He was not the sort of boy I was supposed to marry. The Dutch, they seem very liberal. Everyone thinks they are very liberal. And they are in a way. Very reasonable. Thus, that is what my father is: a reasonable man. And, being a reasonable man, a very reasonable man, he listened to all I had to say very carefully. And then he stopped being a reasonable man and he flew into a rage, a terrible rage, yelling and stomping on the floor, turning red in the face, as they say." Andrea paused to smile.

"Yes. Daddy, the reasonable, liberal man that he was... well."

She paused, looked down at her hiking shoes and at Chester's hand that rested on her ankle. She softly placed her hand on his. "He made me change my mind. He did...I was too young. I was unable to deal with it."

"What happened?"

"Well, I broke up with Federico. You see, I am a very reasonable Dutch girl, too. And I thought - my thinking was - that if my parents would so oppose the marriage, would so oppose everything, then how could it work? It would be very difficult. They were right. I began to think more practically, to think of all the practicalities. All of it was very true. It was true and it was not true at the same time. The main thing was that I let them control me. I was not ready to stand on my own. On my own two feet. Is that how they say it? I still needed their approval. I still needed to know what's true. But now, I tell you, I don't care anymore what is true and what is not."

"So, you didn't go with Federico?"

"No, I did. I mean yes. I did! I went with him. But it was not with all my heart. For my heart was still in my home in Amsterdam. So it did not take a very long time before I returned. And then I did not stay with my parents for long either. Several months perhaps. And then Feddi came back to Amsterdam once again. It was a very crazy time. Very confusing. We lived together for a while. We had an apartment near the Prinsen Gracht, one of the canals. It was such a lovely apartment, full of sunlight. We were thinking at first that we would be able to make for ourselves a new life. But it was over. The moment that I was unable to decide, that's when it was over."

"Uh huh."

"I left home after that. One week or two weeks after that. After Ferdi left," she stated, looking down at her hiking boots.

"I traveled a great deal of traveling. Sometimes with friends, sometimes alone.... First I went to Paris, then to Lyons. I stayed nearly a year in Lyons.... Well, I met a lot of men. It seems I always meet a lot of men, but never are they the right men, men who are good for me.......Present company is excluded," she added with a sudden smile.

"Well, then I went to Israel, where I worked on a kibbutz for two years. That was very nice. After the cold and the grey of Europe, Israel was wonderful. I loved it there, even though I was not Jewish. I don't know why I left there, I should have stayed. I could have married there. Several men were offering marriage to me there. But I went home. I suppose I had to go home. I suppose I'll always have to go home. To Amsterdam. Have you ever been there? No? Anyway, I returned there. I think that every woman and man has a place to which they belong. Usually it is where they are born, that is the simplest arrangement. So I return to Amsterdam. It's my home after all, whatever that means. But as you will have supposed, and as you see, I did not remain for long. That city it calls me and then it boots me out. It was no good. It is the problem I am talking about. So, as a result, always I am needing to move, to travel. Ever since that time I have been moving. And yet.....yet my father cannot forgive me, and I myself cannot forgive myself."

"For what?"

"For ruining my life, for not following his word, for being a bad girl, I don't know exactly. I am not what I am supposed to be. It's more than just conforming to the rest of society. It is a matter of succeeding, succeeding in his eyes. And in my eyes, as well. He still loves me, my father. I know that. But it is not the way that he wants. And it's not the way that I want either. I don't know. It is very confusing."

Chester swung his feet off the log and stood before Andrea. He removed his gloves and placed his hands on her face, covering her eyes with his palms, caressing her face roughly. He dropped to his knees to bring his face on a level with hers. He kissed her deeply on the lips. She closed her eyes and allowed him to kiss her, to restore her. To a new place. Yes, she thought, I am in a new place.

"Come," he said softly, lifting her up, "let's walk up that path. I want to show you something. There are some wonderful trees just around that bend. Come."

He led her along the path around the hillside to another hollow, an opening where the sunlight cast long beams of white-yellow light on a small grove of trees. They were tall redwoods and sugar pines, nothing exceptional about them. But their aspects, the way they stood on the snow-covered hillside, their roots far down into the earth and rock, the way they stood in opposition, in juxtaposition, to each other, the angles of their giant trunks and branches - as well as their size and vitality - imparted to Andrea an excitement, a feeling that she was in a new world, the world of the trees. A blessed world. And all the days that had come before, all that had happened, all that was wrong for her, was indeed past. For today was a new day. There was no past, only a future. Thanks to this Chester. This new Tony.

"You know, these trees have been here for hundreds of years," he stated in a low murmur, as if sharing a confidence. "They're not like people. They don't need to travel. Everything is right here. No trips to Paris, or Lyons, or the kibbutz in Israel. They have to stay here. They're kind of stuck with each other. Talk about home!"

'Yes, but it's a very beautiful home."

"Yes, it's beautiful. But it's not always so easy. When the wind blows it's not so easy here. And then it snows, and it freezes, and the animals chew holes in the bark, and then people come around and just chop them down. It must be difficult to be a tree. But still they grow so beautifully. Look at them. They've created a forest, a world where they live together, in one single spot. So when they look so beautiful like this, when they grow together so nicely, it's a sort of accomplishment. They've had to struggle, to stand up to the wind, to reach and scramble for the sunlight and the water, and stand up to the winds.

And they couldn't decide to pick themselves up and travel to a kibbutz in Israel either. It's like a history here. I'll bet they have very deep memories. Not like ours, I don't think. Probably something different. Deeper. Their roots go down so deep. They must have wonderful memories - which isn't necessarily a good thing. It's a bit of a burden. Because, you know, I had no memory for a while..... It's funny. Just as I was starting to get used to the fact that I had no memory, and I was starting not to worry about it, that's when I started to remember. And I've been remembering things all the time now. And let me tell you, its no great bargain. I think I've had enough with all the remembering game. The trees, though, have a different way of remembering. After all, they have no brains. Maybe it's in their roots. They certainly have a pretty good way of going about things. Look how beautiful they are!"

"Chester?"

"Yeah?"

"Chester, I think you would make a very fine tree," she laughed loudly.

"Yeah. But if I were, then I couldn't do this!"

With a flourish he leapt up onto a big fallen log, took two big strides and jumped out in the air, arms outstretched, landing waist-deep in a snowdrift, flopping on his back, laughing riotously.

Memories

It was only three or three thirty in the afternoon, but the light in the cabin was so meager that it felt like dusk. Andrea pressed the small brass button on the little bedside lamp, which illuminated a small spiral notebook that lay on the night table. She carefully took it in her hands and slowly opened it. On the first page was written the single word Memories in a large, careful, calligraphic script. She began to read with the relish of a child munching on forbidden fruit.

Memories

March 8, 1997.

Memories are flowing out of me from a hidden source. The source is what you would call my self. I can feel it. I can feel my self. And I can feel the memories rushing up on me. The path - the chemical code, the electrical circuitry in my brain - has been concealed from me, or blocked, for a very long time. But now it's all starting to flow. The memories are now coming. They spill out. They rush though me like the stream that races down through the gully after a big snowfall: the days begin to warm again and the water is released from the cold earth. I ask myself how the water got there, i.e., how I got to be me, and how I got to be in the state I'm in now. And then I ask what is the origin of the gravity, the gravitational force, the life, that pulls us all down the hillside. And then the questions as to the origin of the eyes and the mind, the perception that can witness everything. How is it we are able to wonder and talk about ourselves and about this beautiful world? Funny how even these questions are like water. They seem to just wash through me. Something in my body or mind has a way of matching and corresponding to what I see in nature. Who knows? Who knows where it all comes from? Who cares? It's just there after all. A given. A mountain. A continent. It is just there. What I want to say here is that this world is so beautiful my heart could burst. And that should be enough for me. It is. I am thankful, God. I am thankful......

But I am writing down these memories just the same, because I still want to try to make sense of something. I guess I'm human after all. I'm me: L'etat, c'est moi: Chester Knowles, born in 1952 in Los Angeles, the son of Herbert and Sally Knowles, the second of two sons, the husband of Marsha-Sandler Knowles, the father of Vicki and Laurie Knowles. An architect by trade, although I still can't remember where it was I worked. It was a big office, though. I remember the office perfectly. There are simply some names that I can't seem to remember just yet. There are still a great many gaps in my recollections. Gaps of time. Especially most recently, the most recent period. I still don't know how I got to be up here, here in these mountains.

I have begun to remember all sorts of things, a flood of memories. I'm just writing down as much of it as I can. These memories are not at all sequential, and they have no particular logic that I can figure out. They just come. Often they run together in interesting ways, though.

My first memory:

Two weeks ago. February 22, George Washington's birthday, I was sitting out in the woods on my favorite rock. I sit there nearly every afternoon after lunch. The weather was overcast, sort of misty and grey. It looked like it might snow again, but it didn't. The wind was pulling across the upper branches of the big firs. The trees were starting to sway, to respond to the wind in that way that they have that reminds me of horses pitching in to haul a wagon, digging in, setting to work. And that wind - or maybe it was motion of the trees - reminded me of going to school.

I was about seven or eight years old and I was walking to school together with Tommy Shea. We were walking on Normandie Avenue, which was a quiet street in those days, not too many cars. Other children were walking on the street as well - with their backpacks, canvas backpacks, and with their metal lunch pails, which they wagged and swung as they approached the chain link fence of the schoolyard. This was the picture that came to me so clearly - and interestingly it came from the feeling given to me by those tall trees swaying in the wind.

I then experienced a rush of memories about the school: the pale green enamel paint, the linoleum-tiled hallways, the bulletin boards. I remembered a big, glossy poster of Bucky Beaver, the Ipana toothpaste hero that was tacked up on the bulletin board on the first floor, advising us kids to brush after every meal. Tommy Shea would always whisper to me "Brusha, brusha, brusha," as we passed along the hallway, and I would always laugh, and I remember the day Mrs. Neill sent me to the principal's office for laughing out loud in the hallway.

I remember the principal's office very clearly: the high counter, the picture of George Washington high up on the wall - looking down at us kids. Also the mimeograph machine along the wall by the window spitting out it's inky copies. That black ink always got all over my hands!

I remember very clearly the office secretary, Miss James. She would operate that machine like a mimeo master, cranking steadily and patiently on the big long handle. And she never got a smudge on her! When I was in fifth grade I was made office monitor, and I got to crank that handle nearly every morning for Miss James. She taught me how to use the machine, how to stack the reams of paper, how to collate the pages, and she was remarkably patient and sweet with me. No one else was ever so nice, certainly no teacher. My hands, though, would always get all full of ink. So, when I was finished cranking out the mimeos, Miss James would help me wash the ink off my hands in the big sink. She was beautiful, Miss James, although I can't remember exactly what she looked like. She was a Negro, though, and I guess that's what made my feeling of attraction for her all the more exciting. She was my first love. The first time I can remember being attracted to a woman, although I don't think I knew it at the time. I can clearly remember the curves of her body. She was "curvy". I remember the feel of her full body leaning against me as she held my hands under the water. The sensation of her soft, ripe curviness is the essence here. That is how these memories are. They cluster around a sensation, or a feeling.

There are many more memories of the school; they came to me as I let my mind return to the hallways. The doorways were painted in heavy layers of aqua-blue paint. My teachers, I remembered them too: In Kindergarten I had Mrs. Oakley, and she was all right. In first grade I had Mrs.

Fine. The joke that year was: "How's your teacher?" "Fine. Mrs. Fine!" It's still funny to me. In second grade it was Mrs. Neill. Third grade I had Mrs. Frank, who was a terribly mean person. I had trouble recognizing and admitting that fact at the time. My brother, Stan, had Mrs. Frank two years before, and my mother knew her and liked her. Everybody else kept telling me I had to like my teacher. I remember struggling with it. I knew I had to like her, but I also knew that she was mean - a dissonance that was hard for the mind of a boy to make sense of. I remember that very clearly. And I know, I remember, that I experienced that same unsettling, confusing sensation throughout my life whenever I encountered unjust situations, or things that just shouldn't be. It always felt the same. It still does. The way I felt about Mrs. Frank was the way I felt many times in my life. It was a sort of template. So once I have re-captured a feeling, I remember not only one incident or period of my life, but a whole set of similar, nearly identical, experiences. In a certain way, they really are identical experiences. The settings may be altered, but they are all felt in the same way. Like neurological shortcuts.

More Memories

March 10, 1997

There have been many more memories. The next day, as I sat there on my big rock in middle of the snow, I remembered my entire childhood in one wonderful afternoon. The weather was growing colder, and a fine, thin, icy snow began to cover me, but I didn't care. Because the awareness of seeing myself again was tremendously exhilarating. I was very alert, very energized, and I could recall everything at will. Actually, it wasn't something I willed, but something I could feel coming, something coming from outside of myself. I was keenly aware of what was happening to me though. I felt like some child. I was that child. I remembered myself and actually experienced myself at the same time.

I knew that I had gotten lost. I had forgotten who I was. I had lost my self, or rather I had lost the history of myself - the history and chronology of events. My inner self, the thing inside of me that is me, was never lost. That's the main point here. There's a certain kernel, a soul that stays with you. The rest, the history, the personality, is only an objectification. Not to belittle it, we need it. I certainly need it. I miss it. Living without a personal history is like playing a board game, monopoly or cribbage for instance, without a game piece. You can only watch the game, but you can't play. That's how I was when I first got up here in the mountains. That's how I still am really: just watching things all the time, unable to join in the game.

The world sits out there before us like food on a plate. I'm being drawn to it again. Drawn to try to understand it! As I say, there are many questions that I wish I could answer. It's like magnetism the way I am drawn to these questions. And there are no answers to some questions. I don't believe, for example, that I could actually tell anyone what my self is, where it is, where it went, where it will go, etc, but I do know that I know what my self is. I simply cannot put it into the right kind of words.

In any case, that afternoon, sitting out there on the rock, half-covered with the fine snow, well, it was just a wonderful day. The memories began to come to me in a totally real way, and I saw myself as a child: in school, out on the baseball field, out in the sun, or in the YMCA gym playing basketball: full-court games, running, running, running up and down like a little madman, going for lay-ups, sweating, feeling so alive. Then I was walking home, hanging out on Normandie Avenue, taking showers, having dinner with my folks, the familiar 6 o'clock Knowles' family dinners. I was sitting at the table with my parents and my brother Stan again. All the fights and discussions we had at that old wooden table!

Then, in my memories, I was suddenly older, a teen ager, driving the Plymouth, that big green Plymouth, up Santa Monica Blvd, the smell of the upholstery, the feel of the steering wheel. On and on. The memories go on and on. They seem to go on endlessly now. I can recall a ton-load of sensations and details, a flood of details, but above it all, or beneath it all, there was ME, growing up. It was like a movie. I saw MYSELF, the little boy. And I saw him as he grew up. And I felt, and I can feel it again, that the basic soul of that boy is still with me. In fact, it is the main thing that is with me now, for I had forgotten all the trappings, the trimmings, and ways of my later life. For now that I am remembering the details of what I suppose is my life, all I have really is the little boy, the boy who grew up, which is MYSELF. I could write it all down, each memory. But what would be the point? I don't need to prove anything to myself. Or do I? Perhaps I do. I do know that I've been totally occupied the past few days taking notes. Pages upon little pages of memories. Scraps of paper, which are piled up in front of me now that I write. I don't know what to do with them anymore. When I first wrote down the memories they were fresh and alive, and I think writing them down helped me to remember. But now they are already old hat, old business for me. I know them already. What's the point in saying them again? I've noticed more and more, especially up here in the mountains, that people talk way too much. Once something is said, it's dead. But one thing I do want to note down is that the process of remembering is a very physical thing.

In college they had us read Marcel Proust: The Remembrance of Things Past. Well, I can understand him now. It's a very powerful experience to remember experiences from your childhood. Because you remember things only if you hook up to the emotion that you had at that time. The remembering I had was overwhelming for a while. But now I can see that it's a bit of a trap. I could wind up like poor Marcel Proust sipping chamomile tea all day long and getting all excited over nothing. In fact that's what I did almost all of last week. I remembered things and felt them and relived them like Proust, the poor bugger. Except I drank coffee instead of chamomile. But all that is neither here nor there. Who cares about Marcel Proust anyway? My task here is to live. Not just to remember.

I need to return to the world. I'm just not sure about the how and wherefore, and all the other details. But, then again, I don't suppose I was able to plan out my life when I was younger either. And I don't suppose anyone really plans out their lives. They just like to think that they do. When you're a phantom it's easy to see all this. Being alive is a gift. It's all gravy. After all, I was dead. I had thought, or someone or something (my personality?) had thought, that my life was over. But now I am alive, still alive, once again alive - even though I have a different face and body. I still don't know how that came to be. Perhaps that's one of the questions that will remain unanswered. All that's important is that I'm alive. Je vive, donc je suis.

The woods here are so beautiful. There is beauty everywhere. The world is beautiful. But a certain inevitable kind of cruelty is going on at the same time. In the weather, in the living and the dying, it's all very cruel. Nature is cruel and generous at the same time. Woody Guthrie has a line: "This world is such a great and a funny place to be. The gamblin' man is rich. And the working man is poor. And I ain't got no home in this world anymore."

The white snow falls softly in the woods, and collects ever so silently, so slowly on the limbs of the trees. The snowflakes accumulate. But some of the branches finally grow too heavy, and they crack and tumble to the ground. The beautiful white snow has killed them. Perhaps they were weaker branches - survival of the fittest. Natural selection is inherently cruel. The wind attacks and tears at the trees and mountainsides with a vengeance, as if there were an old score to settle. A giant tree, a sugar pine, crashes violently onto the ground. The cold air vibrates, the chipmunks and squirrels suffer the terrible sound. A whole world is gone. Plants are crushed, animals die. A space is left, but it will soon be filled. Any debris is carried off by water, eaten. Everything eventually gets eaten.

March, 11, 1995

I stopped writing there. Now it's the next night and I'm writing again. I think I need to finish off what I started to say. I was talking about the cruelty of the world, the death. I suppose a psychologist would say that I'm obsessed with the subject of death. But that is not true. I am only obsessed with Nature (why do we spell nature with a capital n anyway? Because, truly, nature is like a god). Well, Nature is full of death. Life and death: there is both harshness and beauty in nature. They co-exist. It's hard to put it all together and embrace the whole thing, the whole enchilada, the good and the bad, the life and the death. As for my own death, and now this second life into which I have apparently entered, I simply do not understand it, nor will I try to understand it any longer. It is something that I can't understand, so why waste any more time? I've discovered that it is more wonderful to be living. And maybe I want to live because I can see so much dying go on in the forest. That's what I want to say.

In any case I am alive here, so the question to be asked is: What do I want to do with this life? Do I want to do anything at all? Soon it will be spring. It will be beautiful, it is always beautiful. It's a joy to watch. But I realize that I can't just watch. All of the animals, all of the plants, have a purpose, a job to do. They are all trying to do something: perform their tasks, find their places. They all imagine, I suppose, that their tasks are important. They think that they know what they're doing. But they don't. Their real tasks are known only to God. He creates the rhythm, the rhythm that you can feel sometimes, this sense of unity, this beauty.

I've gotten religious since I've been in the mountains. or maybe it's since I discovered I was a phantom, someone who is alive inexplicably. In any case, I suppose I have definitely become more spiritual. What that means I can't say either. I can only say that I want to be a part of God's unity, a part of the beauty. I think you have to call that unity religion. When I was younger, when I was Chester Knowles, I didn't think so much about the religion. It was science that explained everything for me. I thought science could, or would, explain everything. Pretty stupid, but that's how I was raised. That's how everyone was raised back then in the fifties and sixties. Everything was Science. So I studied to be an engineer, or maybe a mathematician. In college I majored in architecture, and then I got a job drawing plans one summer. So I became a graphics planner, a designer for Hughes - there, I've remembered it, the name of the place I worked at. I was an engineer. But, over the years, I lost the passion for the science. I acquired a love for the art, a feeling for things beautiful. But it was just a hobby. And never did I make the connection between religion and art. Between God and Beauty. But, really, how could it be any other way?

March 14, 1997

A memory of my family. My girls: Vicki and Laurie. I had started to remember about them on other occasions, but yesterday was something different. Yesterday, while I was eating lunch, their faces actually came to me. I felt I was actually with them. Perhaps it was the warmth of the dining room where I was sitting, as well as the familiar comfort of eating, that made me recall them to my mind. The sensation of just sitting peacefully and happily during a meal had that effect on me - and it made me think of them. My heart began to swell. I believe my whole body changed. It was more than just a memory. I'd remembered them before. It's not that I was remembering them for the first time. This time, this memory, was something different. It was as if I were hugging them. It was as if I were there with them. Or, as if they were here with me. It was so powerful I got lost. I suppose I was losing my mind, and it was by no means unpleasant. If insanity means losing the distinction between the real and the unreal, then I guess I was going insane. By no means was it unpleasant, however.

I apparently began to cry and to talk to myself, and who knows what I was saying. I assume I was talking to myself, because the two salesgirls from the souvenir shop, the twins, Mary Lou and Susan, came over, and they kept asking me what I was saying. When I awoke from my memory, or my vision, they were shaking me by the shoulders. They insisted that I try to drink some water. They were right. The water brought me back to myself right away. All the same, I cried for quite a while there, as the girls stood by with their Styrofoam cups (they were both holding

Styrofoam cups of water, the two twins each holding a white Styrofoam cup of water!). They looked like bookends. I began to laugh. And then I cried once again - out of grief, out of sorrow. It felt great, strange to say. I believe I cried because I was happy, happy just to be alive, happy to be so happy. I looked up at the twins, Mary Lou and Susan, and I loved them. I loved everything. It was really a wonderful moment.

But not very diplomatic or strategic! If you're going to be a phantom, you have to lay low, maintain a low profile, keep your nose clean, and stay out of trouble. I made too much of a scene. They were really worried, the poor girls. Apparently they were considering calling for emergency help. To sum it up, I made quite a scene that day, and I'll have to be more careful with this memory stuff. Even if I don't really go insane, I could still wind up getting admitted to some closed-facility nuthouse somewhere. I can just imagine how well the explanation of myself as a phantom would go over with all the psychologists. They would really have a field day. I might never get out of the loony bin.

There is definitely a distinct possibility that I am crazy. Perhaps I'm imagining all this. Wouldn't that be some kind of joke? To wake up from this bad dream and be lying on my bed. Back in Los Angeles, in my house, in my bed. To wake up to reality. Like they do in the movies. You know, the actors wake up at the end of the movie and discover that everything was just one long, ninety-minute dream sequence.

But no. This is 100% reality. I know it. This life is 100% real. I am not crazy. Not yet anyway. I'm just a bit strange. After all, I'm a phantom. Nobody knows me, and I don't know anyone either. I'm not even lonely. I do know now that my name is Chester Knowles. But then again, it looks like knowing who you are isn't particularly useful, either. I wonder what is.

March 22, 1997

Who am I, after all? I still can't be sure. Where and what is my soul? I've recalled and remembered so many of the events of my life, and I still know nothing. I'll tell it anyway. Then I can throw away all these scraps of paper. On with the show!

I was born in Los Angeles on September 14, 1952 at St. Vincent's Hospital.

I was raised by my parents Frank and Lill, together with my older brother Stan. It was a good childhood. At least that's how I see it now: that's to say, it's full of good memories. I played baseball and later I played basketball. I remember endless summer days playing ball. I think I had a very nice life, looking back at it. And I don't feel so badly about it that my life ended. I have already let it go. Or rather, it is gone from me. In any case, it was a good life, a good memory. Sort of like Jimmy Stewart at the end of the movie It's a Wonderful Life. He realizes that he's been lucky just to be alive, he is glad to be alive, and then it's Christmas and all the glory of the situation comes rising up. Quite a movie. Anyway, that's how I feel.

Marsha, let me talk about Marsha. She was my wife for eighteen years. And we dated for several years before that. Marsha was one of the few women I ever slept with. And we slept together all those eighteen years. We were a unit, a couple, a family. Marsha loved me, but at the end she did not love me the way she had before. It wasn't just that we were growing older, or that the sex grew less exciting. It was something else. I think she was becoming bored with me. Or, that she wanted something else for herself that wasn't me. Something that I could not give her. I never really knew what that something was - and I don't think she knew either. But she was looking for it. She was looking for it desperately. I began to think that she was going to leave me, that she wanted to get away, get a divorce. But she never did that, and she grew more angry and withdrawn from me. Still, she loved me. Occasionally, every once in a while, we would fall in love again. With the sex it would become a delight again. We would both be joyous about it. Those nights recharged me, made me think everything would be OK. And perhaps it would have been. Perhaps we might have been able to build on that love that we would from time to time rediscover. Who knows?

My memories of Marsha? It's hard to think of anything particular. It's all just fused together in her name. I have innumerable memories of her. I remember where we met. It was at somebody's party, Richard Wills'. A graduation party. Marsha went to Grant High School in the Valley, but her cousin Ellen went to Fairfax, so Ellen brought Marsha along to that party. I noticed her because she laughed at one of my jokes. She had a wonderful laugh. I said something about a doughnut being more hole than the sum of its parts. She laughed loudly and our eyes met. I can still see her eyes. They were dark green. Her nose was small and she had dimples. I remember the way she smiled, the way the dimples would appear. Her smile was magical for me. I always loved her when she smiled. She would smile when we were having sex sometimes. At least she used to. Later on, she never smiled so much. She was becoming depressed. Perhaps it is better for her that I'm gone. Anyway, I miss her. I miss everything. And in another way I don't miss anything. It would be very interesting to go back to visit, and emotionally I am drawn to it. I would be like some ghost, though - a phantom - drifting around in my past life, observing, seeing how they are doing. I know it will be silly, but I think it is time to go back. I wonder how Marsha is doing, how the girls are. It pains me to think that they would be sad because I had died. After all, I'm not sad, and I'm the one that's dead. It's as if I have moved to another time and place, and they are fated to remain where they were. It's not fair. Life's not fair, and neither is death.

Marsha and the Psychologist, Dr. Gold

They had forced her to come to this psychologist, Dr. Gold. Forced her! Roseanne, Chester's overweight cousin, the fat thing, had studied family counseling or psychology with this Dr. Gold at the UCLA Extension College out in Westwood, and Roseanne thought the world of her. Dr. Gold had "saved her life," affirmed Roseanne. But if her Dr. Gold was such a great therapist, then why was Roseanne still so fat? And why was this Dr. Gold so fat! Furthermore - and here was the main question - why were all these fat people so eager to help? Why should they care about her anyway? Wouldn't the natural condition be to not care? You know, just to leave people alone. How did these people get into the "helping professions"? Aren't they all crazy themselves? Etc. Etc.

Chester's brother Stan stated that all her objections just proved that she needed help. Psychoanalytic theory and so on. Reactive formation, or over-acting, or something like that. Stan insisted that she needed to get out of her rut. He said that the girls were suffering, too - which was a mean thing of Stan to say, but it was true. Marsha respected Stan so much that she had no choice. She had to try the therapy, she couldn't say no. She tried to put him off, she went to the exercise club, which had been good, but Stan still insisted on the therapy - and this silly Dr. Gold. So here we are. For some she couldn't even begin to say no to Stan. Just say no. That's what they said. Well, she couldn't! That's all.

At the first meeting, the first "session", Marsha had entered the dark office, sat down in a low armchair, and perfunctorily explained to Dr. Gold that she had only come to meet with her this one time. Her brother-in-law had suggested she try some therapy, so she had come. "It wasn't my idea," she told the doctor.

Dr. Gold crossed her chubby legs and responded, "Perhaps we ought to deal with that, then."

But Marsha did not answer her. Dr. Gold reciprocated with "therapeutic silence". And so they both sat for ten minutes without a word. Finally, Marsha raised herself up from her chair, said, "OK, then, bye-bye," and left young Dr. Gold looking bewildered, as she shifted round clumsily in her armchair to watch Marsha walk out the door.

That had been the first meeting. But now, Stan had insisted again, and Marsha had returned for a second meeting. She parked her car for four dollars in the tiny underground garage and then took the elevator up to the third floor. Marsha inspected the empty, little waiting room, which Dr. Gold shared with a doctor - a Dr. Willman, a psychiatrist, another shrink. The waiting room was claustrophobic, a closet actually. Rents in this building on San Vicente Blvd in Brentwood were obviously very high. Marsha plopped herself down in a hard armchair, snatched a People magazine off the end table, put it on her lap, and looked around. The waiting room was weighted with a phony, lemon-oil smell. She examined with increasing curiosity a large, wooden-framed picture on the wall opposite: a charcoal of a woman hunched over in grief. How could they put up something so depressing? Was it to encourage business?

"Marsha?"

The wide, smiling-with-crooked-teeth face of Dr. Gold appeared through the half-open door.

Marsha silently acceded and followed Dr. Gold into the dark office. She carefully sat down on a low, leather armchair, and Dr. Gold, in her beige, rayon pants suit, enthroned herself in the large chair opposite, nervously fidgeting with the crease in her pants as she struggled to cross her little legs. When Dr. Gold finally established herself in her chair, she smiled broadly and said,

"So, Marsha."

A long silence ensued. If there was one thing this fat girl was good at, it was waiting. It would be a battle of nerves. Marsha figured she was going to lose anyway so said:

"OK. Let's talk about Chester."

Dr. Gold paused: "If you like...."

"Of course I like. Isn't that what I'm here for? To talk about my Chester?"

Again a pause: "Do you think that's what you're here for?"

Marsha was silent. She looked down at the beige carpet and took a deep breath. She felt a wave of rage coming on. Why must she always feel so angry? Marsha didn't feel like wasting her time yelling at this woman and her stupid way of always answering a question with another question, as if they were playing a game of "ask me another". A cheap way to maintain control it was. Noisily, she exhaled.

"Yes, Dr. Gold. Of course I want to talk about Chester. It's Chester that .
... It's Chester that....It's Chester that...."

"Yes?"

"It's Chester that died goddammit. He died on me!"

"Yes."

"Yes. He died. He died on me. Chester's dead......... He died on me."

There was another long silence, perhaps three minutes. Marsha slumped forward in her chair, her head hanging down. She began to cry softly.

"Marsha? Marsha.... Tell me about Chester."

"You mean what was Chester like? You mean like what kind of person he was? Or like why he's dead?"

"Tell me whatever you like about Chester."

Marsha smiled. She suddenly felt very good.

"Thank you, Dr. Gold."

"It's all right, Marsha. Now...." Again Dr. Gold shifted in her chair. "Tell me about Chester if you can. Whatever you want. In your own words. Whatever you feel you're capable of expressing, whatever.....well, whatever you think."

"OK, I get it. It's OK," Marsha said reassuringly to the doctor, "I can talk about Chester. I can talk about Chester for hours if you like!" her voice rising.

"It's no problem. You're getting paid by the hour anyway, and the insurance is paying all the bills anyhow... Excuse me. Please excuse me."

Here Marsha paused and took several deep, slow breaths.

"Well.......Chester was my life. Or actually ... it was more like Chester was together with me in what I thought was my life. Because it wasn't really my life. It wasn't. And it wasn't Chester's fault either. I don't want to blame Chester. It had to do with me. It was my fault that I had no life. I knew that all along. I think I used to blame him sometimes for my life, but I always knew inside that the fact that I hadn't found my own life, my own life as a woman, independent of Chester, was my own fault. It wasn't Chester's fault."

"You mean that you didn't find your life as a woman with Chester?"

Marsha paused, looked down at her shoes.

"That's right. That's what I said." Here Marsha paused. After a short silence she continued, "And, well, I still haven't found my life, my true life. My real life, my true self. And I think it's even harder now that he's gone. It's all so much harder without him ... You know, there were times that I wanted to leave him. If I had been braver I might have. I always knew that I needed to make my own life. And I was trying to do just that when he left, when he died. I mean I was beginning to be my own person, my own woman, even while I was living with him. And our lovemaking. Well......It was getting better. We loved each other very much. There were times that I could love him very deeply, very passionately. There was a tremendous bond between us. We had been together for years. I was used to him, accustomed to our life. And we had the family. There were our daughters, the girls. It was its own entity.

"A whole is more than the sum of its parts, but the parts can be more than the whole ... Here, you see where I got that one! From Chester! I mean it's nothing significant, but it's something he said one time. As a joke."

"What was that?"

"Well, it was at a party, maybe twenty years ago. It was the party where we met, I believe. No, I'm sure of it. It was a long, long time ago. Anyway, some guy, a graduate student it was - he was older, and more dignified - happened to say that 'the whole is more than the sum of its parts'. You know, as if he were imparting pearls of wisdom or something. And Chester told him that sometimes the parts are more than the sum of the wholes. And the poor guy turned toward Chester and asked naively, "When can that be?" And Chester answered: "When you're adding up doughnuts!"

Dr. Gold burst out in a sudden squeal of laughter, covering her mouth awkwardly with her hand. She then reached up to adjust the temple of her eyeglasses.

"Oh yes, Chester was funny," continued Marsha with a wide smile. "He was very cute, and he was very intelligent. He was a talented guy. But it never led him anywhere. He would meditate...."

"Chester used to meditate?"

"Well, not like they do today. What I mean is that he would get lost in thought. He was an absent-minded professor. He would get lost in a mental problem, or in a problem with his artwork, or with his drawing. Actually, he could get lost in almost anything. It used to drive me crazy sometimes. He could spend the longest times just sitting there - thinking about something. And this is when the girls would be crying. Or the phone would be ringing. And I would be busy with something. And Chester would just be sitting there in his chair oblivious to the world. I mean, I raised the girls myself. Well, that's not true. It's not true...."

"Marsha, you need to allow yourself....."

"No, that's not it. What I'm trying to say is that Chester was also very important to the girls. Just not in a practical way. It's just that he would often be busy just thinking. Or working on his artwork. Chester was a wonderful artist. And there again, he never really did anything with his art. I think once or twice he sold something. Some of his sculptures we sold one time at his friend's garage sale. But Chester was actually an excellent artist - only he never made any money from it. I just finished putting some of his pictures in frames. I have to put them up. I'm not sure exactly how to do it. You see, he would always do all the repairs and work in the house....Anyhow, what I was saying was that when he was free, when he wasn't busy or preoccupied with his projects, he would be totally involved with the girls. He loved them totally, and they loved him......He loved me too. He did.

What I'm saying was that he spent a lot of time just thinking. That's just how he was. But it did get in the way sometimes. But I'm not telling you very much about Chester. What he was like."

"Yes you are Marsha. Tell me more."

"Do you want me to tell you about our sex life?" Marsha snapped. "Isn't that what you therapists like?"

Dr. Gold edged forward in her chair. "Well, of course, I mean.....if you'd like to.. I mean....."

"OK, then. I'll tell you about the sex. I want to. I want to talk about sex. Yes, that's it........ I tell you, I miss it. I mean, since Chester died I haven't had any. There hasn't been anybody else. There never was. It's always been just Chester for me. I was a virgin when we married. Well, not exactly. Let's just say I was a virgin when we got engaged. I want to get all the facts straight, don't I?" smiled Marsha coyly.

"You were telling about your sex life."

"With Chester," Marsha added. "It was with Chester. Well, most of it. I mean. You see, once there was somebody else. Actually twice. But it meant nothing for me. Really, it was nothing. It was the electrician, who had come to fix the wiring in the bathroom. I seduced him. It was all my doing. He was a very handsome guy. A very nice guy actually. Anyway, he didn't compare to Chester. Chester was wonderful in bed. He was good at sex. He was good at most things. In a mechanical kind of way. I mean, he was mechanical, and he was also very tender. It was because he was an artist that he appreciated the beauty in things. Yes. Chester appreciated the beauty in things. And sex was something beautiful. I mean is. Sex is beautiful. Present tense. And I miss it. It's true. It's true."

"Yes."

"Yes what?"

"I'm sorry, are you angry?"

"No, goddammit. I just miss it. The sex! What I'm saying here is that one part of my missing Chester is my missing the sex. Missing him in bed. Oh my God. The bed! I bought a new bed last week. You see, I thought that...... But it only made things worse. I feel too alone......You know, I used to feel stifled, hemmed in by Chester, suffocated by the marriage. But now, the loneliness, the space, the room in the bed to toss and turn in all night.....It's no great fun. I miss him. Really."

"Yes. It's only natural."

"Yeah, Chester was good in bed," Marsha concluded. "I'll see you next week, Dr. Gold? Same time, same place?"

Dr. Gold nodded absentmindedly.

Going Back

It was late afternoon and Chester was standing on a busy sidewalk in the middle of the city of Los Angeles. He inspected a parking meter on Third Street outside a small coffee shop called The Bagel Place. Four minutes showed on the dial. Andrea was inside talking with her boss, Billy. Or rather her "former boss Billy". She had stopped by to hand in her resignation. To "throw off the towel", as she put it. She had been inside for a long time. Chester looked up and down the busy street. The parking meter expired and the red "violation" flag rotated noisily into position. Sure enough, a meter maid was already approaching. A cluster of pedestrians crossed Third Street and walked toward a modern office building. It was a wing of Cedars-Sinai Hospital. Different people crossed the street every half minute; the traffic lights repeated their cycle again and again. The Don't Walk sign flashed its dull red letters. Then it stopped flashing, and held the Don't Walk signal. The cars had their turn again. Then the sign said Walk and the cars waited. Then it changed again. Don't Walk.

The message in red. This street, this intersection. He knew it! He knew it from the past. He knew it from the night of his death! That was it! The lights had told him not to walk, but he had walked just the same. He felt that he had to walk, that he could not stop walking or stumbling on. And he had crossed this street! Chester stood motionless on the curb, while the people and cars continued to pass by him. The light changed several more times, as Chester remained glued to the spot, incapable of movement. He had stood, or rather he had lain, on the sidewalk, at this very spot, this very intersection, once before. He knew it. And then he had it: the whole thing, the whole memory, the whole missing part of his life. In one great suspended chunk it hit him.

He had seen that Don't Walk sign the same night he had run away from the hospital. He had looked at it from this very spot. There had been the restaurant behind him. And there had been the alleyway. He was sure there had been an alleyway! Where was it though? He darted past the restaurant, and raced down the block. He turned at the corner, inspecting the backs of the stores: the cardboard boxes piled up along the dark walls, the green garbage bins. Suddenly he saw it:

The alleyway........ On the night of his death, or the night of his rebirth (call it what you will), he had staggered across Third Street, and then leaned for support on a parking meter along the curbside, right next to the restaurant. Then he had fallen to the pavement. Alongside him, a little black bird also landed, or perhaps the bird had been there all along. The bird stood for several moments on the curbside to look at Chester. And then the bird had opened its wings and lifted itself up from the gutter, and flown off toward the little alleyway. The bird had led him to the alleyway. As Chester looked at it in the light of day, the alleyway - the service road behind the buildings - looked ordinary. It was an ordinary alleyway. But in the early morning hours last summer, this alleyway had drawn him in like a fly. And the alleyway had saved him. Chester now remembered the night, the night of his death - his last night.

He had stumbled into the alleyway, collapsed, and finally crawled along a bit more until he found a spot against a wall, laying himself down onto a big sheet of cardboard. He gasped for breath for perhaps a quarter of an hour, and then he was calm. Perhaps he had slept. He sensed, he knew, he could feel, that his time on earth had come to its end. He opened his eyes to look out one more time at the world. He wanted to see the world one more time before he left it. Even if the world was only an alleyway: "Thank God for the alleyway". He remembered thinking that thought. He thanked God for letting him see the alleyway. Immediately, a remarkable scene unfolded.

The light was meager, but, lying on his side, his cheek resting on the cardboard, he could see everything clearly as if it were day. There was a car parked with its motor running forty or fifty feet from where he lay. It was a shiny white Jaguar. Two men stood alongside the car and talked in hushed tones. One of them handed a package to the other. It was nothing special, but yet it was fascinating. Chester had the thought or feeling that he wished he could be a friend to these men. Suddenly, one of them, the taller one, began to run from the car. Directly toward Chester. Running. The man was only ten feet away when a gunshot blasted the alleyway with sound and light. The man, who was thin, with long white hair, crumpled spastically and fell to the ground with a thud right in front of Chester's face. Fresh red blood gurgled and oozed from his chest onto the asphalt and onto the cardboard as well.

Almost immediately the other man was there - a short, younger man - poking at the body of the dead man, searching aggressively through his pockets. He was right on top of Chester. Suddenly, the man stiffened, stuffed his gun into his jacket pocket, and dashed back to his car, flinging open the door, and speeding out of the alleyway. Perhaps thirty seconds later, police sirens were wailing, and flashing red lights filled the alleyway.

Chester found himself standing. Apparently he had been standing all along. He leaned back against a door - which opened. He found himself inside a dark room: a kitchen or washroom. There were mops and metal pails in the corner. The door clicked shut, and Chester pulled the latch. He held in his left hand a fat manila envelope. He slumped down to the concrete floor and instantly fell asleep, using the envelope as a little pillow.

At dawn, sunlight entered the little chamber through a skylight. It was a utility room with a big, metal washbasin mounted on the wall. Chester stripped naked and doused his body with cold water. He soaped up a large bar of Ivory soap, which he found on a shelf over the sink. The room was cold, but Chester didn't mind. He felt fine.

He toweled himself with a big white apron, which hung on a hook alongside the sink. On a stainless steel counter top he spotted a stack of waiters' uniforms neatly laundered and starched. He took a pair of black trousers and a clean white shirt, but was unable to find any shoes, or socks. On the floor next to the door was a manila envelope. Opening it neatly with a butter knife, he eyed a thick stack of money. Fresh green 100 dollars bills with their pictures of Ben Franklin. Chester slid the envelope with all the money into his pants pocket, quietly opened the door, and peeked out. Carefully he stepped in his bare feet over the white chalk figure of a man, which the police had drawn on the sidewalk. The cardboard was no longer there. No one was there. It was pleasingly quiet. The hazy morning air retained the night's chill, as Chester proceeded barefoot in his waiter's uniform down the dirty alleyway and out onto Third Street. The hospital complex loomed across the street. Chester paused briefly, and decided to walk east - towards the white light of the sun. He needed to move toward the warmth. The street was empty of pedestrians. The stores were still closed. An occasional car passed. Chester walked for half a block. His feet were cold and hurting. He needed to stop and think. He stood in front of a restaurant called the Bagel Place, but it was closed. He approached, and peered through the glass door into a narrow, dark room. He could make out the outlines of wooden chairs stacked upside-down on the tables. He turned to look across the street at the hospital again, and felt a shiver.

"I need to get out of here. I need to move," was his thought. A bicycle rider wearing a backpack glided quietly by and nodded good morning. Chester began to walk east, crossing San Vicente Blvd, and then the big intersection at La Cienega.

He knew where he was: outside Beverly Center. He was on Third Street, he was in L.A., in the heart of town. He had been here dozens of times, hundreds of times - in the past. But now he felt lost, as if he were here for the first time. Things were familiar, yet they were totally new. He could not remember anything clearly. He was lost, really. He was lost in a city he knew. He was alive, but he was as good as dead. He felt tears in his eyes. His feet were burning and cold at the same time.

There was a Rexall's store across the street. Rexall's had been there for years. It had always been there. Recently, though, it had been been modernized. Good old Rexall's. It was open. The sign said it opened at 6 AM. Rexall's had re-done the place. It was quite attractive now. Chester opened the glass doors, stepping onto the rubber mat and then the warm carpeting. He wandered through the quiet aisles looking for some shoes, or a pair of sox. He soon saw that they didn't have a clothes department, that they didn't sell any shoes, or sox either. He did find a pair of plastic slippers. However, when he went to the cashier to pay, he had only a hundred dollar bill, which he held out awkwardly. The young clerk took a step back, but soon smiled broadly and looked Chester in the eyes. Naturally, he could not change a hundred. "Would you have something smaller?" he asked with a sly, but engaging smile. Chester grinned and said, "Well, thanks anyway." He returned the plastic slippers to their place on the shelf. He walked in his bare feet through the Rexall's, and exited at the corner of La Cienega and Beverly Blvd. Cars were beginning to appear in numbers. The street was becoming noisy. Chester turned east again, and walked toward the white sun.

Several blocks away was a coffee shop, Jan's, which was open. The cashier, an older woman with bleached-blond hair, eyed Chester in his waiter's uniform and bare feet. She turned away when he looked at her. A sign in the aisle said Please Wait To Be Seated. Chester waited for several minutes. The cashier was not going to look at him. Chester turned and left.

He was back on Beverly Blvd., a street he knew well. He stopped to look about him. It was all strange, foreign. Where was he? He realized that he could not remember ever having been on this street before. However, he knew it!! It was Beverly Boulevard. He stood motionless in the middle of the sidewalk. A delivery man walked by, staring at him. Chester was crying profusely. He didn't know where he was - at least he couldn't put it into words. He didn't know who he was. Well, he knew who he was, but he couldn't remember his name. He tried to speak, to call out. A strange tone resonated in his throat. He had a different voice. Something had happened to his voice! The feeling of strangeness was frightening. He began to walk again. He was suddenly very hungry. His feet were raw. He was lost. He kept walking east toward the white of the sun, which now appeared as a small globe through the morning clouds.

Several blocks down, his eyes met those of a homeless man who was lying on the red plastic bench of a canopied bus stop. Propped on his elbow, the fellow patiently examined Chester as he walked past.

"Hey, Jackson," he called, "How 'bout a pair of shoes? I got some good shoes, I got some sweaters, I got ...."

"Shoes," answered Chester, turning around.

"Aw' righty then. Let us, then, check out the world-famous shoe department, my man."

And the young, dirty-blond, bearded man slowly rolled off the bench and hoisted himself up alongside a large, metal, shopping cart - which was jammed to overflowing with all sorts of packages and objects. Inside the cart and overhanging the sides were dozens of plastic shopping bags. "Let's see then," he chirped, as he rummaged through the bags.

"There we go! The shoe department. The ol' shoe department. Say Jack, do you have money? I mean I don't want to ask any personal questions so early in the morning. Say, do you know what time it is? Hey, man, you know you're my first customer of the day...."

"Yeah, I got money."

"Well, let's see. You look like at least a size ten and a half." He reached into the cart and pulled out a pair of beat-up, high-top sneakers. "How are these, my man? G'head! Try them on. They're Nikes. Have a seat. Try 'em on!"

Jack sat on the plastic seat, which was warm, and put on the shoes, which were very large. They had no laces. Chester stood up awkwardly.

"A perfect fit! And I'll get you some laces. Hold on a minute." He plunged his large, gritty hands down into the shopping cart. "You don't mind if the laces don't match so perfect-like? I mean like this ain't no Standard Shoes."

"Nah, it's OK." Chester reached into his pocket, found the envelope, and removed a hundred dollar bill. He held it out toward the bearded salesman.

"Whoa. Whoa, my man. That's some hefty currency for so early in the morning. Tell ya what. You can take as much as you like. I got some...."

"No, it's OK. Just the shoes. You can keep the change."

The bearded fellow looked up from his cart and grinned broadly. He put his hands on his hips and laughed.

"Say. I think I have something special for you, my man." And he reached again into the shopping cart. Now he pulled out a pair of brand-new running shoes. They were blue Saucony's, and they had clean fresh laces and they fit Chester perfectly, even without socks.

"They're yours, my man. They were made for you."

Chester laced them up slowly and carefully.

"You take care of yourself," said Chester as he departed.

"No problem, my man. And God bless you," said the young man waving the $100 bill in the air.

A small, yellow sun now rose above the building line. "The sun, what a wonderful thing. And it's always there," Chester thought, feeling better in his new shoes, as he continued east on Beverly Blvd. He crossed Fairfax Avenue and arrived at the big shopping center that sat opposite Farmer's Market at Fairfax and Third. He'd been here countless times before. He knew where he was going without really knowing. At the shopping center he bought an L.A. Times from some elderly men who stood outside the Sav-on Drug Store.

"Paper?" the kindly old fellow asked.

"Yeah, the Times," and Chester handed him a hundred.

"Oh boy," muttered the newsman.

"Is it a problem?...."

"No problem. No problem.... Say Jerry, do you have some big bills?"

Soon they had the change in Chester's hand, the old fellow carefully counting out the bills and the small change, placing it squarely into Chester's palm.

"Excuse me," Chester started in his strange, deep, guttural voice, "do you fellas know where there's a place open for breakfast?"

"Sure. Sure. No problem, sir. The Cleopatra restaurant is open, and they serve a real nice breakfast. Quite a nice breakfast, really." The old gent motioned toward the small restaurant mall. At the rear end of a narrow courtyard was the restaurant. Bold signs in red letters on the windows advertised the breakfast and lunch specials. A goodly number of customers, all of them elderly, were already seated inside the restaurant, as well as at the plastic tables set outside in the courtyard. Sipping coffee and reading newspapers.

Chester ordered the #5: two eggs with home fries, toast, and coffee. He sat down at a table toward the back, and opened the LA Times. The headline read 'Clinton Unveils Economic Plan'; the Sports section read 'Dodgers Lose a Tough One'. Chester stared blankly at the newsprint, and recalled that he usually had the paper delivered to his home. At the doorstep. He recalled how he would bend over to pick up the newspaper in the morning.......outside the red door. But where was that? Where was his home? He knew he had a home! Where was it? Something was very wrong. Chester took a bite of toast, and sipped his coffee. He started on the eggs. They were sunny side up. He remembered that he used to like them scrambled, too. He began to think of all the ways you could make eggs, but then realized that he couldn't recollect any particular restaurant or place he had eaten them. He could recall no specifics. He again considered the fact that he didn't know where his home was. And then he became aware of the fact that he didn't know his own name. He looked around at the restaurant, and regarded all the old folks at their tables. He was clearly different, clearly out of place. He needed to think, he needed to walk. He rushed out of the restaurant.

Chester spied a public bathroom off to the side. It was a dark, dirty room, with wet concrete floors. The place smelled from Ajax and from urine. There were dirty, streaked mirrors above the sink. Chester splashed cold water on his face for a long while. When he raised his head and looked at the mirror he froze. The indistinct reflection opposite him was not him! It was another man! A man with white hair. Chester spun around to look behind him, but no one else was in the room. He placed his face close up to the mirror. The man there, the man that was him - was someone else!

He gripped the edge of the metal sink, and lowered his head. A tremor passed through his shoulders and down his arms. He tried to calm himself. He shook his head repeatedly. There were no thoughts, no words. He dared not look up at the mirror again. He pivoted and marched out of the bathroom, passing the plastic tables and chairs which cluttered the arcade. The old people still sat drinking coffee, reading newspapers. It was a normal day. A regular, summer day. No one looked at him. Chester strode past the dark, still-closed K Mart store, and half-ran down Third Street.

Several blocks down he found a large park where joggers and walkers were doing their laps on a gravel path. The park overlooked a large basin, a ball field. Chester found an empty wooden bench.

What was the use? He didn't know his name. He didn't know where he lived. He didn't know anything, or anyone. Nonetheless, he knew who he was, even if he had no name. The bushes behind the bench sent forth a familiar bouquet. He knew that aroma from summers past. It was so familiar. This park, too, was familiar. The baseball diamond was familiar, and the people were familiar in their way. They were people, just people. The scene was familiar. It was all just there, or it was all just a dream. What was the difference? What was the use? He found himself weeping, his tears falling one by one onto the dry, brown dirt at his feet.

The joggers and walkers gazed at him as they passed, but no one ventured to speak to him. What was there to do? He was alone, no longer a part of this world. Chester rose to his feet, and followed the gravel path. The sneakers were very comfortable, and it felt good to walk on the gravel. The sound of his steps was reassuring. The path led him back out to the street. On Third St., in a large parking lot behind the department store, a group of people were boarding a large chartered bus. He got in line behind them, and then stepped up onto the big, warm bus. Maybe he could go somewhere. He found an empty seat. The other passengers were older people, what they called senior citizens. Chester sat quietly as they eyed him suspiciously. When the driver mounted the steps to the bus he approached Chester directly. He leaned over and spoke in a low voice.

"Listen, buddy. This here is a private charter and everybody here has paid up in advance. So, I mean, I'm going to have to ask you to get off."

Chester reached into his pocket and pulled out his stack of bills. He handed the driver a hundred.

"Listen man, I ain't got any change," the driver exclaimed in a high voice. Leaning closer he added, "But, I mean, if you want to ride on the bus as a private passenger. I mean, it's OK. It'll be all right. Don't worry about it." He pocketed the bill and added a friendly wink, as he stepped back to his padded chair. He efficiently started the engine, and began to busy himself with a stack of thin yellow papers, which he attached to an old-fashioned clipboard. He made several garbled announcements into a microphone. Chester considered whether the driver was speaking in a foreign language, and, if so, was it Armenian or Russian? Chester was falling off to sleep. As the bus pulled out onto Fairfax Avenue, he found himself dreaming about a beach. He was being summoned by the beach. The waves surged up and came to a rest at his feet. They said, "Come with us, come back to the sea. You don't belong here anyway." Chester answered them defiantly," Yes I do! I belong on the land. I'm not a seal or a fish. Here, look at my feet. Look at my new sports shoes. Sauconies. I belong here. I want to stay."

The waves returned to the ocean. But then they came to him again, called to him, pleaded with him, all the time chanting a familiar melody. It was Ain't Misbehavin' by Fats Waller. But played very slowly. Somehow the melody and swelling of the ocean matched the heavy, swaying motion of the bus on the freeway. Chester entered a deep sleep. When he awoke, the bus was pulling alongside a truck-stop diner on the outskirts of Bakersfield. "Twenty minutes, everybody," announced the driver officiously. Chester stretched his neck, rose up from his seat, and filed out with the other passengers.

He filled a large Styrofoam cup with hot coffee, but, when he reached the cashier, remembered that he had left the envelope with his money - all that money! - on the bus. He carefully placed the container next to the coffee machine, and turned dejectedly from the counter, when one of the passengers, a flabby, elderly woman with bleached-red hair, touched his arm with a firm hand and said, "Come, young man. Let me treat ya to a coffee. Come. Let's sit ourselves down at that table over there."

Her name was Sophie, and she explained that she was traveling alone.

"Do ya think I'd be traveling' with any of these?.......Them old hags over there?" she explained, gesturing with her head disparagingly at the other passengers - most of them elderly women - who were seated at the booths across the aisle.

"No way, Jose," she continued. "I travel by myself. Who needs them old hags?"

Chester leaned across the formica table and asked Sophie where the bus was headed.

Sophie paused and examined the young man opposite her. Her eyes focused on him like a crow's.

"Ya mean ya don't know, eh?" probing ever more closely. She pursed her fat lips and fiddled her fingers on the formica table top. She leaned forward, and spoke in a low voice.

"Well, what ain't none of my business, ain't none of my business. I don't know where ya come from, and I don't know where yer goin'. It's not really my business, like I say. But I can tell that you're coming from a very far away place. Europe maybe. Maybe Aizier, or Affica. And I can also tell that maybe you're in a bit of trouble. And it ain't naturally my affair to know where you're goin', nor do I have to know. I only wish you good luck and good fortune. Everything good to you, you should be healthy. By the way, where we're goin' is to the Sequoia National Park."

"Sequoia National Park?"

"Yeah. You know, where them big trees are."

"Yeah, sure."

"So, if ya wanna get lost up in those trees, well, I guess that's your business. Now, hurry up with yer coffee, 'cause the driver'll be callin' us to get back on the bus."

They arrived at the park after noon. The passengers marched into the cafeteria straight away. Chester found a trailhead at the end of the parking lot. The big trees loomed before him. As he ascended into the woods, he turned to look again at the bus in the parking lot below. Sophie stood off to one side. She was watching him. She blew him a kiss, then turned and walked slowly toward the cafeteria to join the others. Chester turned back to the trail. He walked on a sandy trail up the wooded hillside, entering further and further into the world of the trees.................

Chester could recall the feel of the forest even now as he stood on the busy city street. The traffic noise was dreadful, the smell of the cars noxious, almost evil. Yet he could still remember the smell of the trees. The world of the trees was so much better for him. What was he doing here anyway? That's right, it was Andrea who had brought him here. And yes, it was his family he had come to see. He was back in L.A. For better or for worse, he had come to look at his old life again - if only just to look. Funny, now that he had recalled the missing part of his life - the piece that he had missed so much - now that he had it, it was no longer special. It was just another piece of the past. True, everything fit now, everything made sense. He was Chester Knowles, and logic and rationality could again take over. But they didn't. There was no satisfaction in explanations anymore. Instead, what remained with him was simply a longing, a longing for beauty, and for freedom. A desire for beauty: for the mountains, for the sun, the ocean, for the trees, the birds, even for the people. There was a rhythm and beauty that called to him - a beauty that called to him. He could almost hear it. The beauty was everywhere. Chester could stay in LA; or just as easily he could go anywhere. He only knew that he wanted beauty. He wanted the feeling of the forest.

The mountains had called to him so clearly. He savored the memory of how he had stepped down from the bus and proceeded directly up that sloping path - and then deep into the cool stillness of a grove of redwoods. It had been a wonderful moment for him. He recalled with pleasure their immediate hold on him. The quiet of the woods. The way the sun's rays would filter down through the high branches, the way the breeze would pass through the pine needles........

Andrea had come out of the restaurant, and had placed her hands on his shoulders; she was shaking him gently but insistently. He peered into her green eyes. She looked worried.

"What's the matter Andrea? Is everything OK?"

"Everything is OK. I'll tell you all about it at a later time. But are you all right? You were just standing here swaying and smiling like someone crazy."

"It's OK. I was just thinking about the trees."

"Oh, Chester. You are a tree. A tree what walks and talks and says silly nonsense."

"That's true. But real trees have the sense to keep quiet."

"Well, you keep quiet then, and I'll tell you about my plans what I want to do. And then, maybe, you may wish to join me. Well, we'll see. Come let's go to my apartment. It is only right here. Two blocks of walking."

Chester and Andrea

"What is the matter Chester? I have many things to tell to you, but you are dreaming again!"

Chester lay on the big Futon bed, his hands clasped behind his head.

"It's allright, Andrea. It's just that back there, outside the restaurant? I remembered some things. Actually I remember a lot. And now all the memories, the whole of my life is fitted together. I mean, I have the main picture now. The main picture. I almost know how I came to be your friend Tony. Really.... Well actually, I don't really understand quite that much at all, but I do know where and when it all occurred. I know the details, the particulars. It's interesting. Of course, it's still a mystery. I guess it always has been a mystery. You just don't realize it. Still, you get feelings, intuitions, very strong feelings. It would be very valuable, useful, I don't know. I guess I'm still going to have to find out the how..... Andrea, do you know what I'm talking about?"

"Chester, you would be much better doing if you would to be a tree. You are very funny." She leaned down to nuzzle her head against his neck. "Come, let's take a shower."

As she dried her hair, Andrea told Chester about her "planning". She was going to buy half of the Bagel Place from Billy, who was about to default on his loan.

"You see, we returned exactly at the right time. You were correct about the time, Chester. We have returned exactly at the correct time and moment." She kissed him softly on the lips.

Her $25,000 would purchase a half interest, a partnership, with Billy. Tomorrow she would meet with the lawyer. Could Chester come with her to the meeting? Would Chester like an interest in the restaurant, too? Would he like to work there?

Chester's eyes soaked in her beauty, barely listening to the words she was saying.

"Sounds good, Andrea, but I want to ask you a question. Have you thought of moving back to Amsterdam? They have restaurants there too. You could open up the first bagel place in Amsterdam."

"Oh, they have bagel places there already! Bagels are all over Europe."

"Andrea, do you know when the whole is less than the sum of its parts?"

"No"

"When you're adding up bagels!"

"Ach, Chester. That is what we will call the new restaurant: the Whole Bagel. Yes, yes. The Whole Bagel."

"How about if it's a kosher bagel? You could call it the Holy Bagel."

"Chester, do you think you want to be in business with me. A partner? I am aware of what you are calling your special situation. And I am not even too much angry any more that you tell me you have a wife with children. After all, you are a phantom with a special situation. Yes, that's what you said. Well, then everyone would be a special situation. At least to their way of thinking, don't you think so, Chester? Anyway, what I am trying to say to you, Chester, is that maybe you want to be in business with me. That way we can stay together for a while longer yet. And I am telling to you seriously, that you would make good money if you did invest in the restaurant. So what I am saying, all the same, is that we could be partners. In the way of business partners......"

"You know I have to leave you," Chester interrupted sadly. "But I do love you. You know I wish you everything good in the world."

Andrea turned away, stepping into the hallway to put on her clothes. When she returned she said:

"I love you too, Chester," she whispered as she moved toward him, and put her face to his. "I love you and I know you're going as well."

The Return

When Chester returned to his family they did not recognize him. As he advanced up the familiar flagstone walkway and approached the doorway he reached into his left pants pocket for his key. And halted - as he realized that he had no key to this house any more, nor to any house. He knocked softly on the red door, admiring and remembering it at the same time. He saw the new lock he had installed. How long ago had that been? He tried to calculate where the time had gone, and while he was ruminating, Laurie, his six-year-old, ran to the door and asked, "Who is it?"

He answered, without thinking, "Dad." But she did not recognize his voice or hear him through the door, and she shouted "Whaaat?" to him from behind the other side of the door. His heart suddenly turned inward and wrenched. He somehow got the words out of his throat that his name was William, a friend of her Dad's from New York.

After a long pause, Laurie firmly said: "Well, I don't know you."

Chester smiled sheepishly. He touched his fingers to the door.

Meanwhile, he heard his wife's voice and she called to him through the peephole, which he had also installed the same afternoon: "Who is it?"

"It's Willie," he cleared his throat and responded. "From New York. A friend of Chester's from Fairfax High. I don't think we ever met. We were all friends together. Chester, me, Bob, Tommy Shea. I heard about what happened and I was sorry so..."

When Marsha heard him mention Bob and Tommy Shea, she opened the door. He must be who he said he was, though she had never heard of a friend called William. The man at the doorstep was tall, with angular, handsome features and striking, snow-white hair. A nice-looking guy. He looked younger than Tommy, Bob and the others. Younger than Chester. She held the door open, but this William just stood there. His grey eyes, which were a bit crooked, or cross-eyed, glistened with tears.

She looked at him questioningly, and, after several moments, motioned for him to come in. He remained at the threshold. He had played out this scene in his head repeatedly for the past several days, but now he felt unready, embarrassed, uneasy, and ashamed. He felt his face flushing, he must be as red as a beet, he thought. He raised his hand to his cheek, and looked at her. Marsha had lost some weight, she looked a bit drawn. She had cut her long, brown hair, and now she wore it curled under. It looked good. She smiled tentatively, in a friendly way.   Chester   slowly entered the house, stepping into the foyer with great care. Marsha had not recognized him. She did not know who he was. It was true. She did not recognize him. He felt sorry for her; she had been left out. He reached out to touch her shoulder, he turned to embrace her. However, she deftly moved back, passing her hand over her forehead to clear her hair, stepping around him, and at the same time motioning him to enter the house.

"Come on in, William."

Marsha had always been tremendously graceful. She smiled at him her wonderful, familiar smile. Her little nose wrinkled. She was not afraid of him, and apparently felt warmly toward an old friend of Chester's. He felt tears in his eyes again. But then he thought of what he had to do, and his feelings changed, or shifted, almost instantly. He needed to act like his old friend, Willie Miles, and this task now engaged his entire attention.

"I'm sorry," he said, still standing awkwardly under the arched entrance way to the living room, "I know it's been months since Chester died, but I only heard yesterday from Benny (he knew that she didn't know Benny), and I was coming out to Los Angeles today, so I just thought that I'd stop by.... I know we've never met... I mean..... well.....We've never met, but I've heard a bit about you from Tommy."

And then, turning to Laurie, who stood silently looking up at him, "And I've heard that Chester had two very beautiful daughters. Well, this girl is certainly very beautiful. Extremely beautiful!" (Chester knew that Laurie liked the word extremely from one of the storybooks he used to read to her).

At this Laurie smiled one of those little smiles of hers, pinching down the corners of her mouth, her blue eyes laughing. But she refused to talk. Chester thought his heart would explode from happiness. Laurie suddenly spun, her hair flying behind her, and scooted up the steps to her room. Marsha touched him on the arm and ushered him into the living room. Chester moved so slowly that she needed to coax, almost prod, him over to a couch, they had a new couch. She had removed the easy chair, his favorite chair. Chester wondered where she had put it. Perhaps upstairs in the bedroom. Perhaps she had thrown it out. Chester sat down on the new couch and began to examine the room with a hungry curiosity. The house looked different. Very different. Marsha had hung up several of his drawings. They looked very good in frames. The small table in the hallway, the one that held all the newspapers and magazines, was missing. He became absorbed in observing the details of the walls and ceiling. The old cracks and fissures in the plaster presented a familiar landscape - like one's memory of the map of the United States.

Marsha caught his attention. "Um.. May I get you something? Would you like something to drink?"

"I'll have a tea."

"Sure. Excuse me for a minute, William."

"Willie... Everybody calls me Willie. Or just plain Will."

"OK, Will," she smiled, leaving the room with her usual grace. Even though he had been clumsy, she had been graceful. She looked beautiful. Her body was thinner, tauter. She seemed a bit older, but somehow even more attractive. While she was in the kitchen, Chester began to consider whether she had met another man. Why not? How could I stop her? What right would I have? After all, I'm only a phantom. For all I know, he thought, I might not even be real. This may just be a game, an invention. It's like a fairy tale: An Arabian Nights story: Aladdin's three wishes. And the first of his three wishes, albeit an unconscious wish, one that even he himself was unaware of formulating, was this very one: to visit his old life again, perhaps even to return to his old life...Wouldn't that be wonderful? Chester leaned back and examined the ceiling again.

Chester considered the problem that his awareness of the situation had little effect. Whether he was aware or unaware of what was going on, whatever happened happened. His awareness was of little consequence, not a factor. His emotions would seem to matter, but perhaps even his emotions were a preordained aspect of the situation. His awareness too could be just another feature that was preordained in the same way. There would be no way to verify anything. Dream could be reality, and reality dream. Or simply a wish.... Chester looked up from his reverie. Laurie was standing in front of him, wiggling her bare toes and feet into the carpet, biting down on her lower lip with her front teeth, suppressing a smile.

"Say, what'cha got there, dreamgirl?" he said in a hoarse voice.

She just stood there, fidgeting a bit, but gazing straight into his eyes. She didn't recognize him. Her eyes were smiling, though. He wanted to reach out and grab her up in a big hug. Like he always did. But this time it wasn't like always. Laurie didn't even know who he was. Still, she must like him, he thought, because she had brought out her favorite doll, called Little Sis, the one he had bought for her at Toys R Us two years ago for her birthday. She had loved that doll immediately, she used to sleep with it. Perhaps she still did.

Chester felt his voice choke when he said, "That's an extremely nice doll. Such...er..... a nice doll! What's her name?"

Laurie stepped forward and thrust the doll at him. He slowly took it in his big hands and pressed it to his stomach.

"I know this doll. It's called Lil Sis. Right?......Yeah," he continued softly, "I know this little sister girl."

Laurie's eyes lit up. "Yes. And look! She can talk. She can talk really good!"

"What does she say?"

Laurie was silent again, looking down at her toes. Then she moved closer, alongside him.

"She calls for her Daddy," she spoke softly but distinctly.

"Is Lil' Sis sad?"

She nodded slowly, but then added eagerly, "But I tell her: 'Don't be sad, little sister. Your Daddy's up in heaven, and he's looking down on you.'"

Marsha returned to the room with the tea and a plate of cookies.

"Is everything all right?"

"Yeah sure," he answered, "We were just talking about....... We were talking about Chester."

"Oh," said Marsha with a note of concern. Marsha placed the tray of cookies very fastidiously in the center of the coffee table.

"It's all right, Mommy," perked up Laurie. "I was showing the man how little sister talks about Daddy. And how it's OK. How it's good to talk about Daddy, like you say. You said so, remember? You said that....."

"Yes, I know what I said. But maybe Willie doesn't want to talk about it. Willie was Daddy's friend, you see...."

"Did you play together?" Laurie twirled toward him with her little, impish smile, her tiny teeth biting again on her lower lip.

"That's right, Laurie. We used to play together." Turning to Marsha he said, "Yeah, that's right. I knew Chester a long time. A long time ago." His eyes were teary, but he was smiling, beaming with a joy that was difficult to suppress.

Marsha gently moved the tea on the coffee table in front of him and put her hand on his shoulder. Her hand remained there for a long moment. Without thinking, he pressed his cheek against her hand and wrist. She looked down at him and smiled. It was an unusual situation. But it was quite all right. This Willie really did seem like an old friend, almost like family. It was strange. She found him lovely. Endearing. The way his beard bristled against her hand. She bent over and kissed him on the head, on his snow-white hair.

Chester felt a surge of emotion in his blood. There was happiness and fear at once, a general and total excitement that charged his body strangely. He had felt this feeling before when he had remembered his family up in the mountains. Above and beyond the emotion of the moment was an additional electricity, yes it was electricity, a charge, running through his limbs and chest, indeed centering in his chest, on his breastplate and collar bone. Yes I am really dead, he thought to himself, and these emotions I am feeling are being transposed upon me from another place, from heaven. He stood up. He faced Marsha with a sudden strength. He looked into her eyes - they sparkled, they were so lovely, they were even more beautiful than before. She looked questioningly at him, as if looking for an answer. Naturally, she looked at him as if she would look at another man. But not just any man. Her look was one of encouragement. Chester knew that he could love her all over again.

"I'm sorry. I'm just so sorry. I can't explain it," he stammered.

She tilted her head slightly and continued to gaze at him warmly.

"I'm sorry," he said, "that he had to die so soon. I mean I'm just so sorry for him. I'm sure he was very happy with you. I'm really sorry for him that he had to leave........ And, well........"

She said something which he didn't hear clearly, though he was sure that she spoke his name, and then she silently stepped forward and embraced him softly. She was crying, too, and leaned on him in her familiar way. Chester's hands hung at his sides. And then he felt Laurie's little head leaning gently on his hip. He placed his hand on her head, and he wept openly. The size of his heart seemed to expand to include the entire living room, and then he had the exquisite sense that his sorrow was like a light, also extending and permeating the room. After several moments, perhaps longer, the feeling of expansion faded. He now felt his body palpably. He was back to normal; his arms were still holding his wife and his daughter, his feet on the carpet. He remained standing, and he held them firmly. His usual hesitancy was gone. Perhaps, he thought, he was a man again, more than just a phantom. He was real, even though he was no longer Chester. He was a new person, this Willie perhaps. He was in grief, he was in sorrow. He was living. And it felt very good. Whatever was happening, it was alive, it was giving him life.

It was more than just the pleasure he could obtain when he observed the world, when he could see and experience the beauty of the world. This pleasure, this state of excitation, it came from being a part of the world, from being seized by the world. He was back into life. The world was revolving around him, swirling. He could feel the feel of Marsha. He could tell that Marsha needed someone. He thought: "I've left her all alone." Laurie, on the other hand, seemed a wonderfully self-sufficient creature. She would be all right.

They were drinking their tea, when Vicki opened the front door and, eying Chester suspiciously, proceeded up the steps to her room.

"How is Vicki doing?" Chester asked Marsha in a soft voice.

Marsha paused, leaned back in the sofa, and looked again at Chester.

"You know Vicki? How do you know......"

"I guess Chester told me.... Well, never mind. I'm sorry I asked....."

"It's OK. William. We've all been having a rough time. It's been very rough. And I know that I myself haven't even begun to grieve for him yet. I'm just beginning to deal with it....Deal with it, that's my therapist's words: to deal with it, to deal with things. Everything's a big deal. You see I'm going to a therapist. Yeah. Actually, she's not a bad person. I think she means well. But Vicki........ Vicki......I suppose that Vicki has been grieving, grieving in her own way, and that's normal, I guess. It's only natural. She's kind of turned inward. Tonight I sent her out to her friend's house, the neighbor two doors down. She barely goes out anymore. She didn't want to go tonight, either. So now I suppose that she's angry at me.....Seems she's always angry at me.....Laurie, go up and tell Vicki to come down for some cookies, OK?" Laurie skipped across the living room carpet, her eyes on Chester.

Chester sat down again on the couch and said:

"Well, they seem like good girls. And that's the main thing.... that they're good. Chester told me about them a bit...."

"What did he say?"

"Oh, not too much. He once told me a story about how ....Just how much he loved them. I think that he really loved you, too. Very much. He must have. I know it. And I want to tell you this, Marsha. That I ......I mean I'm only an old friend of Chester's, and of course I hadn't seen him much in recent years, but, Marsha, if you need anything, you just call me. Whatever I can do...."

"Thank you so much, Willie. You've really touched me."

The girls were galloping down the steps.

Vicki entered the living room together with Laurie. They were holding hands. They both grinned shyly at Chester. Chester wanted to hug them both. He wanted to fall to the floor and hug them.

Marsha spoke, "Vicki, I want you to meet Willie, one of Daddy's old friends...."

"Actually, I'm not so old," joked Chester, "I'm only 95!"

"You're not 95!" squealed Laurie.

"That's right, I'm really only 84."

Laurie bit down on her lower lip.

"How about you, Vicki? How old are you?"

"Oh, I'm eleven."

"So, I'm only, let's see, seventy-three years older than you!"

"You're not so old. I think you're younger than Daddy."

"Well..... How about we sit down and have some cookies with tea?" spoke Marsha.

At the table Chester used some of his old tricks on the girls. He made the spoons dance the way Charlie Chaplin did in The Gold Rush. The girls knew the routine of course, and they insisted on performing the spoon dance for him endless times. Vicki jumped up and began to hobble around the room like Charlie Chaplin. Laurie laughed so hard she bubbled tea through her nose, which set off yet another wave of laughter. Marsha and Chester laughed with the girls and let themselves absorb the joy of the children - Marsha glad to see some happiness in the house again, and Chester glad just to see them, to see them happy. Abruptly, clumsily, he made his exit, waving shyly to the girls. He felt overwhelmed and fatigued. And he was afraid he would make a mistake and confess his identity. Marsha rushed to meet him at the door. Their eyes met, and Chester apperceived that their parting was romantic. Marsha looked up at him. Her green eyes were open and unafraid of him. And he felt excited - as if he were falling in love. He knew he had to leave right away. He grasped her hands, and mumbled some awkward words about dropping by again.

He rushed down the dark, tree-lined street, which he knew by heart, and tried to calm himself. He inhaled the cool fresh air; he could identify the bouquet of their neighbor's jasmine bushes. He knew this street so well. But, somehow, he was walking here for the first time. Everything was for the first time. The smell of the jasmine bushes was for the first time. He had met Marsha for the first time too.

Marsha and Dr. Gold

Marsha sat in the tiny waiting room, and tried to suppress her smile as she admired the large David Hockney print on the wall opposite. She had presented it to Dr. Gold the week before to replace that gruesome charcoal drawing. Dr. Gold had accepted the gift reluctantly, insisting at first that she "just couldn't accept it", that she "could lose her license", that it "wasn't exactly proper". But she had hung it up! Marsha had changed her mind about Dr. Gold. She liked her. And she was eager to meet with her now.

Dr. Gold began by ceremoniously crossing her cute, chubby legs. She began directly:

"So tell me, Marsha. Have you thought about what we talked about last session?"

"Well no. Well, yes and no..... Listen.... I have something to tell you. I've met a man. He's one of Chester's old friends, someone I never met before. But he showed up last week. Kind of all of a sudden. Out of the blue. And, well, he's very nice. We've made love. And, well, I wanted to tell you about it."

"Uh huh."

"Is that all you're going to say? One of your 'uh huhs'?"

"OK then, Marsha, if you'd like to tell me about him....Please .... What's his name?"

His name is Willie, Will. And he is someone special. And, well, what's strange, what's really weird is that, well, he's kind of like Chester......Well, not like Chester exactly, but there's something about him. Maybe because he's Chester's friend. I don't know."

"You mean that...."

"I mean that when we had sex, when we made love, it felt like Chester inside. And I know that sounds strange, like I'm crazy. I know you'll say that I'm imagining, or projecting - isn't that the word? Or displacing, or just plain fantasizing. But I swear he's like Chester. Like when Chester was younger. He has white hair, but he's very young in spirit, kind of like a child. The way he experiences things, the way he enjoys the sex, the way he seems to enjoy everything. Like a child. He has a sort of enthusiasm, an interest, a fascination, in everything. He's really someone special. And he came to me like a gift. That's why I say he's like Chester."

"And do you have any thoughts about his ability to make a commitment? Or your own ability to make a commitment?"

"Commitment? Who's talking about commitments? Jeez, I mean if he's gone tomorrow it will be enough. We're going to the beach tomorrow, though. He says he wants to take the girls out."

"Take the girls out?"

"Yes! They really hit it off with him, too. He just loves them."

"It sounds very nice, Marsha," Dr. Gold stated.

"'Yes it is. It's more than nice. I mean I can begin to feel things again. I think you can understand that. I can feel things again.......oh yes, it's definitely very nice."

"Yes, I suppose. But don't you think we need to think about....."

"I'm sorry, Dr. Gold. You know, I've come to enjoy our talks. Very much. But right now, there's no need to analyze anything. Do you know what Will told me? He was talking about trees...."

"Trees?"

"Yes, trees. Sequoia trees. He said that he wants to takes us up there to the national park to see them. Anyway, what he said is that a tree has no thoughts."

"Well, of course...."

"And what he said was that he couldn't decide whether it was a higher or lower state of evolution - or state of being - to have no thoughts. Whether it's better or worse. And what I said was that it's probably a lot better off for the trees to have no thoughts."

"Well, for a tree, perhaps....."

"For us, too," continued Marsha emphatically. "What good do thoughts ever do us anyway? Usually, you're just thinking the same thoughts over and over again. You worry. You obsess. That's the word, isn't it?"

"Yes, obsessing. Or, obsession-compulsion."

"Yes, a compulsion to think.......Anyway, Chester, I mean Will, thinks it's overrated."

Chester and Marsha

Chester had thought earlier in the day not to come, to cancel somehow. But he arrived at the house at seven, and presented Marsha with a bouquet of flowers, which seemed to please her very much. Funny, she never used to like flowers particularly, or perhaps he had simply never noticed it before. The girls stood uneasily in the vestibule looking at him. Suddenly, Laurie rushed at him and hugged him around his legs. Vicki stepped forward with one large stride and extended her hand. They shook hands stiffly. Chester smiled broadly. He felt himself starting to cry.

"Would you like to come to the table?" interposed Marsha, "Everything's ready."

The table was set with their best tablecloth. Marsha put the flowers in a new vase in the center of the table. A bottle of chilled, white Chianti was opened. Chester thought that he had bought the bottle nearly a year ago at Trader Joe's, though perhaps it was possible that Marsha had purchased it herself. She served roast chicken and potatoes, one of his favorite dishes. After dinner, Laurie started to play the spoon game again, but Vicki chastised her sharply, a bit too sharply. Chester broke the tension with some magic tricks, some new ones he had learned from Bill, the forest ranger.

Later that night, he and Marsha made love. The girls had gone to bed, and Chester and Marsha had sat opposite each other on the living room couches finishing off the wine.

"Tell me about yourself, Will. I asked Tommy Shea about you, but he said that he hadn't seen you for years...."

"Well, that's because I moved to New York, and then I traveled a lot, and well, we fell out of touch."

"But you were born in LA?"

"Oh yeah. Right next to Chester's house. Two houses down - on Normandie Avenue. It was a lovely neighborhood then. I remember how quiet it used to be. I guess that was before they built the freeway. It was a nice time. We were all good friends then. Chester, me, Tommy, Al, Francis. We grew up together. But after high school I went away to college at Berkeley. So, I guess I grew apart from the others. And it was the sixties, and I guess that changed a lot of us. The world, the world around us, just seemed to get a lot bigger, and a lot crazier."

"Yeah, I know what you mean."

"And people like myself didn't know what to do with it. So I wound up moving around a lot. I And I suppose I'm still moving around a lot. And the more I move around, the more I travel, the more it doesn't matter. I mean the place, the location, doesn't matter. Wait.... I want to get this right. What I mean is that the place matters a lot, but that there are so many beautiful places in the world that you can find good things nearly everywhere. The world is good or it's bad wherever you go. I travel a lot still. Recently I was up in the Sequoia forests, the Sequoia National Park. You've never been there. Or, I mean you've probably never been there...."

"No I never did. But how did you?...."

"Well, it's just incredible there. It's just incredible. The way the trees look. You really have to see it. But a lot of places are incredible. Even LA. The mountains here, the beach. That's what I'm trying to say. There are just an awful lot of wonderful places to go. Well, I suppose I've confused you now, Marsha. You must think that I've gone crazy..."

"No. No. Not at all."

"OK then, but enough about me. I don't really want to talk about me. Tell me about yourself. How have you been doing? I mean, since Chester went away. How have you been doing? You look wonderful. I mean, it must have been hard."

"Well it was. It is, Will. It's always hard...... It's... It's funny the way I can talk with you. You seem to have an understanding."

"Marsha, I can't begin to tell you.....I guess it's because of Chester....."

Marsha reached out and put her hand on his. "Thank you," she pronounced.

Chester leaned forward and placed his hand on hers. Marsha placed her other hand on his, and squeezed it with a force Chester had never felt before. Her hands and arms trembled. He placed his lips up to hers. She slowly moved her lips to touch his. Softly they kissed. He shifted over to the sofa, and placed his arms around her. They kissed deeply, her lips parting, as she leaned back on the couch and their bodies began to press together. Marsha pulled back, and examined Chester's face.

"What is it?" he asked with alarm.

"Nothing, Will," she said pensively. "I'm sorry."

"It's OK?"

"Yes, yes," she smiled.

He felt himself smiling, too. She placed her hands behind his neck. They kissed again tentatively, then more deeply.

"Come, Will. I think we ought to go upstairs. That is, if you want to."

"Very much, Marsha."

Andrea and Chester Again

Chester and Andrea lay side by side in bed as the afternoon sun set behind the low apartment building opposite.

"You know, Chester? Chester are you listening? You know, I feel like I am a different person now. Well, not exactly a different person. What it is is that now I feel like the person that I really am.

"Well, you are who you are. Who else could you be, Andrea?"

"Yes, that's it, Chester. What I believe is that earlier, my whole life up till now, I was trying to be someone else, someone I was not. I acted and I did things that were not in my natural way. But now, now I am no longer trying to be someone else. You know, to act in a different manner. Oof, you know what I mean."

"A good girl."

"Yes. I was a good girl. At least I was trying to be a good girl. For my family, for my boyfriends. For everyone."

"So now you get to be who you really are."

"Yes. You know what I mean! Did you have to do that too? As a child? Always to live like that? Like a person who must play to the expectations of others?"

"No. I don't think so - not in my earlier life. I was always just me. I suppose I was lucky. But being yourself isn't always so easy, either. I was too direct and straight-forward in my ways, and people can't always handle that. They prefer to be soft-soaped most of the times. I mean, you need a bit of cunning to get by in life, and I never had any of that. I was sort of incapable of playing games I didn't like. And now I have another body, and everything is starting all over again, and I'm still pretty much the same. Except I'm so busy figuring out what's going on that I have no time or energy to think about what kind of person I should try to be or how I ought to act."

"That's true, Chester. That would be one of the advantages of being a phantom."

"Yeah, I guess. But with you, you were educated to be a certain way - to be a good girl. And the funny thing is that you are. You really are a good girl." Chester mussed her hair.

"You're a good girl without trying to be. You're a good girl anyway. So you don't need to bother trying. And you don't need to be worrying about yourself. You're just wonderful. You know that now, don't you?"

"Ooh Chester, you are like an angel to me."

"Well, I may be an angel, or I might be a bad sort of phantom. I really don't know. It would depend on the situation. But I'm going to be leaving, Andrea."

Andrea slowly shifted her long body out of the bed, and wheeled away from him.

"Oh, sure, Chester. I see it coming. You men are all the same...."

"No, no, Andrea. Don't be like that. It's just something that has to happen, so I'm letting you know. Last night I was with my wife. No, wait. Let me finish. I remembered where my house was! I told you the other day that I remembered everything about my past? Well, I remembered where my home was, too. So I went to visit them. To see them. My daughters, I saw them. And it changes everything for me, Andrea. I'm bound to help them. To be there for them. I don't think I can really return there, but..... I can't begin to describe it.... how it was. But my love has to be for them. And even though I love you, too...."

"Ha! Now you say that you love me. You never spoke like this before...."

"Oh, Andrea. You know that I love you. I'm not forgetting you. I'm not leaving because I don't like you. You know I love you. It's just that you're young. And I am old. And your path is different from mine. I'm a damned phantom. I could disappear tomorrow in a puff of smoke. I'm not someone for you. And I belong somewhere else...."

"I'm sorry, Chester," she demurred. "I know that you are right. It's only that I have fallen in love with you so much."

Chester reached to pull her back onto the bed. He kissed her on the lips and rolled with her until they fell off the mattress and onto the floor.

He laughed, "Say, I said I'm leaving, but I didn't mean just yet. Are you in such a hurry to get rid of me?"

"Chester, you are a very comical phantom. Do you know that?"

Vicki

The shiny green waves rushed and spilled forth onto the smooth sand like hungry, bubbling creatures. Each wave cast its own idiosyncratic outline onto the sand as it was drawn back into the sea. The curves overlapped, intermingled, and faded, soon washed over and erased by the next set of frothy waves, which now raced up onto to their toes as they stood together on the shoreline.

"I used to come here with your father," stated Chester as he looked out at the horizon.

Vicki's head snapped toward him, her eyes suddenly fixed on him.

"Yeah, that's right. When we were younger, we would come here often. Your father always wanted to come to the beach."

"So do I. I like the beach too."

"Well, I guess you're like your father in that respect."

"Yes. I am," she said in a stiff, determined voice.

"You're pretty like your mother, but...."

"My mother's not pretty."

"Oh....well. Well, kiddo..." Chester stopped himself short. "What I mean is that when she was younger she was very pretty. Sort of like you."

Vicki eyed him silently.

"And I'll tell you something else you may not agree with," (Vicki's eyes were still upon him) "You're

going to have to be more patient with her. You're gonna
have to try to be nice."

He continued to face the ocean. Vicki too looked
out blankly at the waves.

"You're the one who's like Chester, so you're the
one who has to help her, to be with her. You're gonna have
to grow up fast. It doesn't seem fair, but a lot of things aren't
fair. Look at this ocean, Vicki. This ocean isn't fair, is it? But
it's a wonderful ocean."

Vicki turned slowly toward him. She looked calmly
and deeply at him.

She said: "You really were a friend with my Daddy?
You were his best friend, weren't you?"

"Yeah."

Chester bent down, picked up a flat stone, and
skipped it out over the water. Four or five times it popped
on the low surf. Vicki turned to gaze at Chester, for he had
thrown the stone just the way her Daddy used to do it.

"Go ahead, Vicki. Let's see ya throw 'em."

Vicki carefully selected several flat stones. She threw
the first one too high, but the second and third throws
skipped a number of times.

"Say, you're pretty good. You already throw them
better than me."

"You should have seen the way my Daddy could
throw them. He was the best in the world!"

"Well, you're pretty good too, Vicki."

Vicki smiled her familiar, squinting smile at him.
Then she surprised him with a quick kiss on the cheek. She
turned away laughing, running and skipping along the shore.

Chester watched her outline against the sun: her hair
flying in the air, flung out by the wind, her stringy arms and
legs, long-extended, and swinging in stride - and he tried to
fix this image of her in his mind. If he didn't see Vicki after

today, this moment of seeing her, this certainty about her strength, would have to suffice.

He turned back to look at Marsha and Laurie. Laurie was sprawled on all fours, half submerged in sand, digging intently. Marsha was sitting on the low beach chair with her legs stretched on the sand. She peered at him over the rims of her sunglasses. She smiled softly as he approached.

"Hi, Willie."

"Hello, my love."

"Willie, sit down. I want to ask you something. I don't know how to say it. But..... You see I was talking with my therapist, and well, she said..... well, never mind what she said......

"What did she say?"

"She said.... Wait. I don't really want to talk about that. Well, OK. What she was talking about was commitment. I mean, I don't like that word either. Stop smiling. Because I don't want commitment or promises or anything, really, from you. But I do want to know something. Are you leaving?.....Well, I guess I said it.....Stop smiling, Will.....It's just that it will be hard for me, and for the girls, too, to never know exactly when you'll be coming back. And I want you to come back. You know how much.... I think I love you. But I can feel that you're leaving again. Am I right?.....No, don't answer me. You don't have to...."

Chester placed his hand on her bare calf, which was warm from the sun.

"Yeah, Marsha, I am. I have to leave. But...... when I'm gone, and I go into my next life, or whatever happens....... I'm still going to love you, and miss you....... Like this ocean here. Whenever you miss me, whenever you want to see me, just come out to the ocean."

Shanghai-ed, Sealed, and Delivered

"Tummie, hey man, Tummie! Look like over der? Like I cannot believe it? Like what my eyes be seeing." Julio edged forward in the car seat and pointed through the windshield.

"Holy moly, guacamole! Like it ain't possible, man. You know what I mean? It just ain't possible fo' it to be happenin'. But that's him, man. It's for sure.... Right, Julio man? It's him. I mean, like, how many white-haired guys are there like dat, that go walkin' around, walkin' around on fucking Third Street like dat? Like they don't know what's happenin' man, like what the fuck is happenin to dem, man? Like everyting's like nuthin'? Ya know whot I mean? Like how many guys are there like dat?"

"Yeah. You're right my man. It's him absolutely. Absolutely. Come on. Let's pick him up, Tummie. I'll betcha Carlos won't be able to believe it neider."

"Yeah man. We better pick him up. Like a package. Like the Federal Express. You know, I almost had a job workin' for de Federal Express? But lemme tell you Julio. It's weird, man. I mean, ya think a guy is dead. And then he is not. I mean, like he's dead, and then he is not? ......Hold on a second....... Lemme just take a little hit before we get him in the car. I mean this is heavy!"

Tummie leaned to the side of the steering wheel and snorted some coke out of a paper napkin. Then he started up the engine of the white Jaguar. They pulled out onto Third Street, trailing closely behind Chester. At the corner of Sweetzer and Third, Tummie hung a quick right turn, and blocked Chester's path just as he was stepping off the curb.

"OK, Tony," said Julio from the lowered side window.

Chester looked behind him.

"Get in, man!"

"You hear him?" added Tummie, leaning over. "He say to get in the fucking car!"

Chester spied the barrel of a large handgun protruding from the bottom ledge of the side window. He shifted his eyes to check out the street. No one was near. No one would notice if he were shot down. These young kids would get away with it. He would die for nothing. ...

The back door of the sedan unlatched with a click and opened.

"OK, Tony. Get the fuck in."

Chester entered, and closed the heavy door behind him.

They drove across Fairfax to the 10 Freeway and headed east, past downtown and onto the San Bernardino Freeway. Chester sat in the back while the kidnappers chatted up front as if he weren't there. Julio had put down the gun, tucked it under his leg. Chester couldn't understand their talk - which was frustrating, considering his position. He wanted to figure out where they were taking him, and why they had taken him. He knew it was related to the Tony business, the guy he looked like. Andrea had explained that Tony had been dealing in drugs. So probably it was related to the $30,000 in his backpack (it was $24,000 now). How was he going to account for the missing money? He'd have to make it up. The back pack lay on the seat next to him. Innocent enough. These kids up front also seemed innocent - except for the gun. He soon found that he could understand their talk a bit. They spoke about various friends they had, and it was mostly nonsense, which was reassuring in a way. They weren't bad kids, you couldn't condemn them.

As they climbed the mountains above San Bernardino, they put on a loud CD of rap music. One of the songs said over and over in an angry voice: "I got the brick. I got the brick." At Victorville, they gassed up and got some hamburgers at a McDonald's drive-through. One of the kids said:

"You like Big Macs, man? "'Cause dat's what we got."

He tossed two paper-wrapped burgers onto Chester's lap. "An' you eat them up good, man, 'cause we don' want you to have no complaints wit de service."

They played more rap music and stopped at the Nevada State line to gas up again. Chester fell asleep, but was roused by Julio after perhaps an hour.

"Wake up, man. Wake up! C'mon. We're in Vegas and we gonna be gettin' ouda de car, so you just stay with me, you hear? We can't park the car here no more. It's all valet now. So, we gotta get outta de car and walk a little. C'mon."

Chester slid over the seat and stepped out into a hot asphalt parking lot. Tummie moved behind him and nudged Chester in the ribs with the barrel of a gun. Julio walked alongside.

"OK, man. Lets go. I wanna see Carlos' face when he see you, man. This is gonna be cool, right Julio?"

They crossed a large parking lot and entered the lobby of a swank condominium complex. They took the elevator to the second floor, as Tummie held the pistol underneath a jacket he draped over his arm. He sharply jabbed Chester with the barrel as they walked into the apartment. Carlos was sitting in his boxer shorts in front of the TV watching a music video. He barely reacted when he saw them, except for a slight squint of the eyes. He put the TV on mute, and leaned back on the couch.

Julio sat down next to Carlos and put out his fist for a handshake.

"Ainch you gonna give us five, man? I mean, can you believe dis, Carlos? I mean can you believe dis?"

"Shut up, man," muttered Carlos, and slowly rose from the couch. He stepped toward Chester and stood facing him. Suddenly he lashed the back of his hand across Chester's face. Chester's nose spurted blood. Carlos smacked him again, this time on the forehead, as Tummie grasped Chester's arms from behind.

"Tie him up in de chair," commanded Carlos.

They bound him to the chair with a roll of mailing tape, while Carlos left the room to shower and change his clothes. From inside the shower he called out,

"You done tying him, Tummie? OK, you can soften him up a little, like to make him talk. But not too much, just like to make him talk."

After ten minutes, Carlos returned, wearing an elegant jeans suit. He ambled past Tummie and Julio, who now stood quietly next to the big glass patio door. Carlos took a look at a bloody, unconscious Chester, stole a look at his two henchmen, and began to pace the floor. Tummie stuffed his hands deep in his trouser pockets, while Julio toyed with his pistol, checking out the alignment of the sites, taking aim at Chester's head. Chester had passed out, his mussed white hair hung down over his chest. Blood still dripped from his face onto his jeans, and a small pool of dark blood had collected on his pants legs at the juncture of his knees. Tummie had punched and slapped him a bit too hard. Chester had offered no information before fainting. He had only repeated: "I'm not who you think I am. I'm not Tony. I'm not anybody. I'm not anybody."

So, Tummie had pounded him with more punches to the stomach and then uppercuts to the head in order to keep him from drooping. Julio had not thought to stop him. So now Carlos was angry, pacing the floor. It was not fair, thought Tummie. Carlos now stepped out on the patio, sat down in the big lounge chair, and lit one of his Cuban cigars. Halfway through the cigar he tossed it down on the green lawn below. He entered the room and ordered:

"OK, you two. Get the bastard awake, clean him up, and then clean up dis fucking carpet. When I get back I want it clean. Clean. I don't wanna see not a speck of nothin'. I'll take him myself. I'll get rid of him. Julio, gimme de keys to the Jaguar."

When Chester roused himself from a deep sleep he saw that he was back in the car, laid out on the back seat. With difficulty, he raised himself to a sitting position to look out the window. They were on a minor road headed south as far as he could tell. The signs said: Route 95, Hoover Dam, Arizona border 18 miles. Carlos turned off onto a dirt road, slowing down to dip and pitch over deep ruts and depressions. He let the car roll to a stop.

"OK, Tony, or whoever the fuck you are, get out."

Carlos came around to open the side door for Chester. He pointed a large handgun at Chester's head. Chester dragged himself out, snatching his backpack, which was on the floorboard by the door. He tumbled out of the car, and fell onto the hard-packed dirt road.

"Get up."

Chester slowly rose from his knees. He drew himself up, and faced Carlos and the barrel of the gun. The sun was setting, outlining Carlos in orange. Chester squinted and peered at Carlos' silhouette. His body hurt and he was thirsty. He saw that he was about to die, but had no thoughts about it.

"Say Carlos, how 'bout a drink of water?"

"What the fuck?"

"You know how it goes at the end of the song? The John Henry song. It says. And Chester began to croon in a hoarse, cracked voice:

"And the very last words I heard that poor boy say
Gimme a cool drink of water 'fore I die.
Gimme a cool drink of water 'fore I die.
Cool drink of water.
Cool drink of water.
Cool drink of water 'fore I die,"

Chester looked directly at Carlos.

"So how 'bout it? How 'bout a drink?"

"Shut the fuck up, man. You talk too much. You're makin' me like crazy."

"You think it's too much of a request? A glass of water? Some guy you are!"

Carlos responded, "Listen, man. Maybe I'm not even gonna kill you. Yeah, maybe I'm jus' gonna leave you out here like this. Out here!" he shouted.

Carlos waved the barrel of his pistol over his head in a wide arc.

"Yeah, maybe I'm just gonna leave you here. Yeah, that's what I'm gonna do."

"Awful swell of ya, Carlos."

"Absolutely, man. Real swell, like you say. 'Cause there be no bullet holes in your ass, when they find you. That is, if they find you." Carlos bared his teeth in a little grin, and slowly turned his head around to pan the barren landscape. "You probably don't make it back, you know."

"Probably not."

"Good luck, A-hole." Carlos stuffed the gun under his belt and returned to the car. He made a broken U-turn and headed back out on the dirt road. Chester watched the cloud of dust rise behind the car until it finally disappeared behind a bend. He couldn't discern the highway anywhere. He sat down on the hard stony dirt. It was sad to be dying. Even if he were to live again, it was still sad. A cool breeze stirred over the ground and up onto his body. It seemed to lift Chester onto his feet, as he stood facing the last rays of the sun.

"Not a bad way to die,'" he thought. "Like in the movies."

He began to walk. Into the wind. Toward the sun.

Marsha and Dr. Gold Reprise

"So you never heard from him again?"

"No."

"And how do you feel about that?"

"About what?"

Dr. Gold did not respond. After a full minute, Marsha said,

"OK. OK. Therapeutic silence over. Actually, it's not a therapeutic silence, Dr. Gold. It's more like you're pouting. Wait.... Don't get angry, I'm only kidding with you. I imagine you can put an interpretation on kidding, too. I can't stop you from analyzing. It's your job, your predilection. But sometimes, there's just not too much you can say.... Anyway, no. The answer is no. I haven't heard from Will. I guess it's nearly a month, actually it's exactly one month tomorrow. I don't understand it either. He was supposed to call. I was kind of thinking that he was going to go with us to the beach again. But he didn't show up. Never called. Never anything... I told you all this already."

"Yes. Last week, Marsha. And, well. Marsha..... Well, it sounds like another rough separation."

"Separation?"

"Well, yes. Another separation....."

"Wait a minute, doctor. Chester died. It's different. I know separation is the psychoanalytic term for it. My cousin, or Chester's cousin, Janice, gave me a few books to read...... But when someone dies, it's just different, Your psychoanalyst friends are wrong about that one. But, I don't want to argue now. I just want to get my feelings straight.

Actually they are straight. I just need to express them, get them out. That's how clear they are. I feel so hurt, Dr. Gold, you can't believe it........ I liked him so very much. I mean.... I mean I loved him. I do. I still do. It's strange when you think about it - that you could come to love someone so quickly. But he taught me that. He taught me to love again, William. He did. And if I don't see him again, it'll be OK, too. Sure, I'd like to see him again. And I regret the separation, or whatever you want to call it."

"And you miss him?"

"Yes! Isn't that what I've been saying?"

"Yes."

"Yes. You say yes, but you don't agree. Why can't you just understand and accept it that I feel OK with it? That I can be sad, and miss him, and be messed up about it, and still be OK?"

"Yeah, Marsha," affirmed Dr. Gold. She got up from her chair. She gestured for Marsha to get up, too. Dr. Gold grabbed Marsha, and hugged her with a surprising force.

"Take care, Marsha."

Marsha's eyes were wet. Marsha gently pulled back from the embrace, and faced her therapist squarely in the eyes.

"Swim on my own. That's the words you used. Yes, one time you said that. Well, don't worry. I'll be OK. Will said that whenever I miss him, whenever I want to be with him, I should go down to the ocean."

Dr. Gold smiled softly.

Alive Again

Chester awoke, and immediately observed that clear plastic tubes were attached to his arms. The intravenous connection provided a saline/sugar/vitamin B complex solution - according to the label on the plastic sac that hung from the metal T hook alongside his bed. A green-lighted monitor behind the bed showed his heartbeat graphically, and on the bottom of the screen, the pulse was indicated. The lights flashed 60, 61, then 60 again. The nodes of the green graph were regular. They fluttered when Chester raised himself on his elbow to look around.

He looked back at the tubes in his arms. He remembered he had yanked them out. Had someone inserted them again? He had left the hospital, hadn't he? He had lived a life, a portion of a life. A year perhaps. Had it been a dream? What about Marsha and the girls? He had seen them again. He was sure of it. The mountains and the snow. Andrea. And the trip back to L.A. And then there had been the gangsters, the drug dealers. They had left him to die in the desert. He had been walking toward the highway, toward the sun. Had it all been a dream?

But, no, this was a different room. It was not the same room. Chester shifted in his bed. The spikes on the TV monitor began to ripple and wave about the screen. He gripped the stainless steel bed rail and tried to calm his breathing. He thought about it some more. If he were dreaming, then his mind could easily have changed the location to another room. Perhaps the hospital attendants had wheeled him out and changed his room while he slept.

Could he be dreaming the same dream twice? And if you could repeat a dream, why not repeat a whole life? What would be the difference between a dream and a life? There was no way to be sure. But this was a different room. He was sure of that. Chester lay back on the pillow and soon was asleep.

He was roused by the nursing attendant, who placed his breakfast tray on the side table. A few moments later, a nurse strode into the room with a big smile and a bold voice.

"So you're up! How yer feeling? Lemme see yer monitor."

She leaned on the bed, as she seized his hand and placed her fingers on his wrist.

"Good. You're doing just fine. How are you feeling? Lemme see here. Your chart.... Hmmm, not much info here...... Wait a minute.....Well, you can have your breakfast. I have to go to the station to check something. You can have your breakfast meanwhile. Wait a minute. You don't have any allergies to any food products? Diabetic condition, special diet? Right? OK, I'll be back in a minute. Enjoy your breakfast."

Chester watched her body, which squeezed tightly into her white uniform, walk out the door. It was a familiar body, a familiar type of woman: short, a bit porky. Most people liked this kind of woman, but Chester never had. He lifted the plastic cover of his breakfast plate. French toast. It was cold. So was the coffee. Chester reached for the tiny container of orange juice, and drank it down slowly, pausing frequently, as it was very cold, with chips and splinters of ice. He sat up in his bed to await the return of the nurse, but it was nearly an hour before she returned - accompanied by an attractive young woman wearing an open, white hospital coat over her blue jeans and designer T-shirt. The young woman was presented as the social worker in charge of discharges. The nurse hurriedly wrote something in the chart, and with a sigh of "Good Luck", delivered Chester to the hands of the discharge planner.

Her name was Natalie Silver, and she hurriedly explained about the "pre-discharge community resource assessment", which she then proceeded to administer. It was an ordinary questionnaire. She began to run through a list of questions about his medical insurance, his occupation, address, family, etc.

"No, I don't have any of those. There's not much sense in asking me all these questions, Miss Silver."

"You don't have any address?"

"Well no, I guess not. Not anymore. You see, I wasn't really in Las Vegas. And I wasn't really in L.A. I wasn't really anywhere."

"Is there anyone you could call that can help you?"

"I don't suppose."

"Well, where are you going to go? Do you have any plan? I mean do you have any friends or family you could stay with?"

"No. I guess not. I guess I'll go to a hotel."

"Do you have money? What about financial assistance? We can make the referral right now..."

"Do they have my backpack?"

"Excuse me?"

"My backpack. Do I still have it? I had money in it."

"Well, I could check with the...."

"Please, Natalie."

He was discharged later that day, walking out the wide lobby of the Las Vegas Medical Center with his backpack looped over his shoulder. He stepped out into the deep heat of the Las Vegas evening. The sun had yet to set on the golden city.

Marsha and Dr. Gold

"So tell me more. That is if you want to. That is, if you feel that...."

"What's there to say? He's back. Again... I mean I saw him again... I mean, he comes and he goes, and I suppose I'm getting used to it. Of course, I wish I knew when he was coming. It would be nice. Like I could circle it in on my calendar. But it isn't like that. Or, I should I say, he's just not like that. And I just accept it. He's a phantom, that's the word he used. So he comes and goes. Although this last time, he said that he doesn't think he'll be back for a while. We slept together again. He's staying at a motel out on the beach in Malibu, but he's slept over a couple of times. He's the most wonderful lover.......And I know it's strange that I say this all the time, but he reminds me so much of Chester. I mean there's something about him that's exactly like Chester, that's what so strange.

And no, I don't want to talk about it - the sex part, I mean, how he could be like Chester. It's just that he's so caring and tender and.....well....I'm glad I saw him again, I'm glad he came back, that's the main thing....... And I have no regrets or second thoughts, or guilt. That's the main thing too. I know you always want to talk about guilt, but no, there's no guilt."

Marsha paused, and leaned forward in her chair:

"There's nothing to feel guilty about," Marsha continued. "Nothing...... And yes, I know it's not going to last forever. I just don't care. He told me that he'd be be leaving. He's just not the type of person who stays, or makes commitments. He's a free spirit. A phantom, that's how he described himself. I asked him one night, after we had made love. We were just talking, laying on our backs, talking. And that's what he said."

"A phantom? What's that supposed to...."

"I don't know. He just said it, kind of like a slip of the tongue. An unconscious slip of the tongue. You like those don't you?"

"Well..."

"Well, that's it. That's what he said. He's a phantom."

Davy

"Well, tie me up and call me Suzie!" exclaimed the big, fat man behind the bar. "'Cause if you ain't come back from the dead, well then, I'm a monkey's uncle. And I don't wanna hear no comments about the resemblance to tha gorillas. How ya doin' Tony? How ya doin?"

Davy extended his big paw of a hand to shake and pump Chester's.

"Man, they tol' me you wez dead, but I didn't believe 'em. I swear it! I just knew you weren't dead. It wasn't your time yet. Every man has a time, ya know that? It's written in the book. At Rosh Hashanna and Yom Kippur, in the Jewish religion, it's written in the book, whether you're gonna kick the bucket or not. Actually, it's God himself who does the writing. Not that anyone gets to see what he writes. Heh, heh. But he writes, he does, and then later, hopefully a lot later, if you catch my meaning, we find out. Not that I believe in any of that rigamarol. Naah….

My father did, though. And my grandfather, and my uncles, all of us, we all used to believe. We would all walk over to schul every Saturdee, every Shabbis. Yeah, we used to be real religious. But that's neither here nor there. Yeah, I know. Old Davy's running off at the mouth again. Well, heck, that's how I am. I'm too old ta change it. Or maybe I'm just too old ta wanna change it. Or ta care what people think about me. I like to talk. I always did. That's how I am. But the main thing here, the main point, what I'm tryin' ta say, is that you're here, doggonnit. Among the living." Davy smacked Chester on the arm.

"It wasn't your time to go yet," he continued. "You must still have some things to do. We're put on this earth for a purpose. And, Tony, you still have to find out yer purpose. Like I wez tellin' ya the last time we met, a young man like you has lotsa things to do. For instance, for instance....Like takin' care of that pitiful, miserable, sorrowful collection of musicians that you call a band. I tell, ya Tony, ya got here just in the nick of time for them boys. They're lost without ya. Forgotten and kaput. You gotta straighten those poor fellas out..... I tell ya, ya look good Tony. How ya doin'?" Davy nudged Chester on the arm again.

Chester grinned and played along with the bartender, who obviously also thought he was Tony. Chester ordered a vodka and lemon, which Davy insisted was "on the house". As Chester raised the glass to his lips, Davy slapped his big, meaty palm on the counter and exclaimed:

"Well I'll be dog-garned if it ain't them! Look Tony, here they come. Ya see 'em? Over there by the roulette wheel. Whattsa matta, ya don't recognize 'em? It's not like they grew up or anythin'. It's your fellas, your troops. I talk about 'em and then they appear. I shoulda talked about the Meshiach. Now, that's one my grandfatha, should he rest in peace, always used ta say...."

"That's my band, huh?"

"Wha? Oh yeah, that's them. Ya know, I got them a job, I did. Down at the Midnight Lounge over near the Holiday Inn downtown. They're doin' all right, I suppose. But still, like I tell ya, they can use a little lift, a guiding hand, if you know what I mean. And, well, I didn't tell ya yet, but I heard that their drummer is gonna quit, so I suppose that maybe they'll be makin' ya an offer...."

The group of four scraggly, thin young men approached, and stopped in their tracks in front of Chester.

"Tony?"

"Yeah it's me. I guess I'm back."

Phantom Memories

October 10, 1997

Memories. I'm still writing about memories. But what are they worth? A handful of sand. Life slips through your fingers, and the more you try to hold onto it, the faster you lose it. Last night I was with this woman, a prostitute I talk with sometimes. We've had sex a number of times, but recently we just talk. She's from Tunisia via Paris, and a number of other places, and I suppose she's been through a lot. She said that she feels like a filter, a paper cone, a coffee filter. She used a French word for it, but what she meant is what's left in the filter after the coffee is brewed. The dregs. I didn't comment at the time. After all, what can you say to that? But when you consider the matter in those terms, in terms of being what's left behind, you'd have to say that we (we ourselves, our souls, whatever you want to call it) are more like the liquid, the coffee that has passed through. It's the memories that would be the dregs.

So the memories for me are back there in the filter. Behind me. I can only talk about what's happening now. I know who I was in the past. Chester Knowles was my name, just as William Morton is my name now. Chester Knowles is history. Back in the filter. I myself am flowing on. I suppose I'm sitting in the carafe at present. Call it Las Vegas.

It certainly is an interesting place. It's perfect for someone like me - a phantom, a man without a face, a man with someone else's face. A man who isn't really anybody. Nobody but myself, for I am 100% me. There is nothing else, no one else. There's no personality, no ego, and not too many frills. Objectively, you'd still have to say that I'm a normal man, with a normal body: William Morton is the name. I have an identity, even though I still don't have a social security card. But what I am, what I really am, is independent of any particular name or identity.

Las Vegas is comfortable because you don't need much of an identity here. No one really looks at you here. They're too afraid. Or too ashamed. Everyone's on the run. They aren't really interested in anyone else. Not to mention the gamblers, because the gamblers are like machines - Pavlovian dogs pulling handles and drooling at the sight and sound of money. The gamblers don't look you in the eye ever. Staying at this cheap motel, I could remain incognito forever. And isn't that what I want? Isn't incognito my middle name? William Incognito Morton. Incognito is my true situation. Unknown. Mort is my situation in French. Dead. The odds that I'll run into those gangsters again are statistically insignificant, but I'm still careful.

I've settled into a life of quiet loneliness and routine. I eat, I sleep well. I work as a janitor in a small office building. I can walk to work, which is good because I still don't have a car. They pay me cash - a lot less than I ought to receive, but since I have no social security card I can't be too choosy. It's enough money to get by on, though.

I'm drawing again. Interesting how that part of me remains constant. I've done some very nice work recently using materials I've found in the mountains nearby. I realize that nothing I draw or sculpt can match the mountains. So why draw? Why sculpt? Well, it's just for my own pleasure.

The mountains and plants and animals all seem to strive toward beauty, so why should I be any different? Why should I need to justify myself? The mountains outside of town have become a part of me, or vice versa. It seems I am living only to be able to go into the mountains on weekends and days off.

Last week up in Red Rock Canyon I had a realization. It involved the proportions between the approximate widths and distances between the hills: the omnipresence of the "golden proportion": 1 to 1.6103. Approximately a 5 to 8 ratio. The geometry and mathematics that lie behind everything has captivated me once again, and set me thinking. Some things are not to be understood, but their contemplation is nonetheless very pleasant. The artwork generated by such a frame of mind is very gratifying.

My life, my work as a person, is also coming along well. I am going down to L.A. next week to meet with Marsha. I will say goodbye to her then. And to the girls. They are doing fine. They miss me. I see that they miss me. It's such a painful feeling to see them. They came out to Vegas two weeks ago and stayed at the New York, New York place. I took them over to the Mirage and introduced them to Roy and Siegfried, whom I had met a couple of times, and they were real nice about taking the girls backstage. We even got to see the tigers up close, which was a great experience for the girls. Of course, they were scared at first. So was I. But it's nice to give them experiences like that. I wish I could give them more.

Seeing the girls is hard for me. Too pleasurable, too difficult to handle. All the emotions are like a rapture, a rhapsody for me. It's like a drug. It pitches me out - or is it down? - into such a strong emotional morass that I am continuously overwhelmed and lost in a state of amazement. And what benefit is there in it for them? I want to believe I can help them, but who knows if I can help them? They seem to be doing very well without me. It's hard to decide what to do. I'm a bit like a surgeon operating on himself, making corrections on his own life. It's no good. I don't know why, but I know that it is no good. I need to let it go too. So I will put an end to it. Soon.............

November 5, 1997.

Several weeks have passed. I ran into the members of Tony's old rock band. Or rather, they ran into me. First I had the pleasure of meeting Davy, a bartender who used to be a friend of Tony's. He thought I was Tony, too. Davy is someone that needs to have a book written about him. Maybe I'll try that in my next life. Anyway, I was talking to Davy when up rushed the members of the band. They grabbed me and hugged me, assuming that we were big friends. Blood brothers, they kept saying.

They apologized again and again for leaving me in LA, and were happy that I bore them no grudge. How could I have a grudge? I had no memory of them at all. And what's the sense of getting angry and holding grudges anyway? When you're a phantom you do get a better perspective on those sorts of issues. So they were glad I wasn't angry and then they asked me about drugs - which they were hoping I could supply the way Tony had. They were disappointed when I couldn't satisfy them. They thought I was lying, or teasing, or deceiving them. I was afraid I would be led back to those gangsters again. I must have acted suspiciously. They all said that I was "paranoid". But they didn't mind much. Getting paranoid is a daily occurrence with them. It's no big deal.

They wanted me to come stay with them and play drums in the band. It seems that earlier that same day their drummer had split. And also that he had taken their stash of drugs. So they thought it a miracle that I, Tony, had returned at this time. Who knows, maybe it was a miracle. Because if you consider that every small event leads up to the next one, and that each event depends on hundreds of ordinary, even silly events, to precede it, then everything is a miracle. That's what they thought anyway. They said it was "really awesome", which I suppose it was. However, I must say that I disappointed them in regards to the drugs.

I wound up playing the drums with them that first night, which I enjoyed very much. We got free drinks and food. The drumming wasn't so difficult, I soon remembered the techniques from my high school days. They wanted me to sing, too. Tony used to play with these guys and he did most of the singing. He apparently organized the group back in L.A. They were very thankful to me for all that I had done for them. Apparently Tony was a very good singer. But I didn't sing. At least not at first. The bass player handled the vocals that night. He's quite good, much better than I am, but since he's so often forgetting the lyrics (from being so stoned all the time), I do most of the vocals now. I'm quitting the janitor job, and I'll stay with the music for a while. It's a lovely way to make a living, and somehow I've fit in with these guys. When I was a teenager, I'd hoped to be a rock and roll star, but this is just a job, another job. But I do like it. I already knew most of the oldies material.

We play some pretty nice songs, and I taught them some new ones - some Kinks songs and some Everly Brothers. It's not real art, but often when we're on stage we can obtain a certain level of emotion and mutual sympathy where the sound comes out just right. I'm reminded of the old Chuck Berry recordings, which sound so perfect. Or the early Beatles songs. I tried to explain this notion of perfection to the band, but they didn't understand it, other than that they can get "a high off the music".

These guys are quite a bunch of Bozos, really. I can't explain why it is I like them so much. They sit around the motel room all day watching television. Toward evening they finally work up the energy to practice their music for an hour or two. They don't play very well either, because they're usually too stoned, or drunk, or just plain tired. For them, being tired represents a sort of spiritual accomplishment. It's cool to be tired and wasted. I just don't get it. There's a generation gap between us. I'm an old man. Whether I'm Willie or Chester, I'm a lot older than them.

There are also two young women, Crystal and Jamie, who stay with them nearly all the time. They claim to have an apartment in town, but they're usually with us, with the guys. No one seems to be having any sex, though. The band - they go by the name The Lone Rangers - rent two adjacent rooms at the motel. They wander in and out, depending on what drugs are available in each room, and depending on what is on TV. Usually each room is tuned to a different show. Possibly the drugs have drained them of their energy and intelligence, although I think it is the TV that is most to blame. Once again, an explanation of the world becomes problematic, and I must remind myself to not try to understand everything. But all the same I am always asking myself what causes what. Are they dulled by the TV and drugs, or are they already dull and thus easy prey? I suppose I just can't get over how dull they are. The other day I entered the room and they were all agitated about that old show, the Hollywood Squares. There was a big to-do over who was the show's smartest, or prettiest panelist - or something like that.

So why do I like them so much? I believe I like them in the abstract, in an abstract way. Sure, they're each different, each has a different personality. And I like each one in a different way. I feel suddenly very protective. I would say I like them - nay, love them - the way I would love a dog or a horse. I can't help but love them and try to help them. They are creatures of God, of nature. And I am another such creature, drawn to them. Attracted and bound to them by love. It's a natural process. An abstract function of the body and mind - whatever that means. I know I'm talking through my hat, but I do know that I've stumbled upon something significant here. We are all creatures of God. When you can see people that way, in that abstract kind of way, it seems that the love and the kindness are not far behind.

The Ocean

Chester stood barefoot on the shoreline, the sun's rays on his back and shoulders; he observed the way the warmth began to sink into and course through his body. The morning sun was well up. The majesty of the sea was plainly evident. Far out, far away, lay Japan and Asia. The salt water lolled, surged, and journeyed over the huge, round globe. The water was a living entity on the earth. The seas and oceans were all one. It was alive, propelled by tides and winds and forces from the center of the earth. Moved by an idea perhaps. The breadth of the rolling expanse filled Chester with a similar feeling of expanse, for the majesty was his as well. He was a witness to this world. He could feel it.

He stepped forth into the cold water, waded out to his waist, and quickly plunged in, diving under the curl of a big, rushing wave. He stroked his way underwater past the surging breakers to the deep and colder water. The cold penetrated his limbs, through to his bones. He felt fine, though, and the cold soon subsided. He swam parallel to the shoreline in long, hard strokes. He turned on his back when he grew tired. The sky was nearly white overhead. He had always loved the beach; he had never realized how much. Things were much simpler now. He no longer needed to explain things to anyone, or justify his actions, or accommodate them to any pre-conceived notions.

He rode an easy wave back to the shore. He found his fresh, white, motel towel and pressed it onto his face. The towel was warm from sitting in the sun. Still holding the towel, he strode back down to the shoreline. The waves lapped their foam on his feet, then they swiftly receded. Tiny bubbles followed their wakes; the bubbles glistened and popped on the smooth sand. Chester peered out at the white line of the horizon. Yes it's definitely round, he thought. How could anyone have ever thought it was flat? It was obviously round. Yet for thousands of years everybody thought the world was flat.

"Everybody's stupid," his brother Stan liked to tell him.

"Everybody's smart, everybody's stupid." That was how it went. Chester smiled. His brother, Stan, remained a positive image in Chester's mind: a feeling of love, an actual physical piece of something. Although he might never see Stan again, he had a piece of Stan in his heart. After all they were both pieces of the same thing: the Knowles family: a droplet in a larger gene pool. Humanity would be represented by a somewhat larger globule in the ocean of living material - the molecules and atoms of which were held together by some force or spirit which made them alive, a spirit which spanned the planet, permeated the waters, reached up to the sky and out to the stars and distant galaxies. Thus, his memory of Stan was just a piece of the whole, as was everything else. To be alive, and additionally to be conscious of being alive, was a fortuitous circumstance. It was all a brief gift, a piece of luck.

Why he was alive again? If there were a purpose to this second life, if there were an idea behind it all, a unifying concept, would he feel any better if he knew it? There was no sense even trying to comprehend the world. Chester had been humbled in this respect. He no longer tried to understand. It was enough just to be alive. Back in the mountains, when he had first woken up from his sleep, he had not been a functioning human being. He had been unable even to follow simple conversations; he had barely been able to talk. But now he had learned to get along a bit.

He had loved Andrea and had helped her. He had helped Marsha and the girls. Helping was no big thing. It was a natural process, once selfishness was gone. Being alive was easy. Being alive was a joy.

Chester looked out over the ocean - the great, salty, freezing cold, heartless, churning, surging, wide-swept, beautiful ocean - which covered nearly all the earth. Chester felt a great love, a longing, for this ocean. He longed for its expanse, its endless fathoms. This sympathy did not belong to him personally. It would remain with him in the next life. Even if he reverted to a handful of atoms, he would still love the sea. Who knew how many his days would be - in this new body? He felt that it would not be too long. No sense getting greedy. Chester quickly turned to collect his things: his towel, his sneakers. As he walked back across the sand, he began to smile at the notion that was turning in his brain: he had nowhere to go. He had no home.

He skipped up onto the piles of large grey boulders at the bottom of the cliff, and then trod up the narrow path which led to the Pacific Coast Highway. The PCH held a lot of memories for Chester. He knew he could remember all sorts of incidents and emotions associated with riding along the PCH in his former life. But he chose not to bother with them. It was as if all the memories went by on a television screen in another room. Chester was skipping them, not minding them.

He stood at the edge of the highway, and attended the fast-rushing cars, that blew past him in big, heavy gusts of wind and noise. He waited for the proper opportunity to dart across the asphalt highway to his motel. Chester unlocked the door to his room. The double bed and formica table greeted him with a dead message, an empty silence. Once he had left the beach, the world had become difficult and harsh. Noisy, heartless, and ugly. It was true that the ocean waves were also threatening. Loud and violent. But the feeling standing in front of the waves was one of awe, and the feeling on the highway looking at the cars and the asphalt was one of disgust. Why must the natural world and the man-made worlds be so different? Man, after all, is just another of God's creatures. It was undeniable, though. The world of today's man was ugly as sin.

Chester dressed without showering. In a quarter of an hour, he had his bags packed.

"Leavin' already?" said the clerk at the desk.

"Yup. I am. I'm.........."

"OK then. Let me see." The clerk busied himself with a computer screen and then with a noisy printer.... "Here we go. You just fill this out."

Chester paid with six hundred dollar bills, which he pulled from a tattered manila envelope. The motel clerk looked up from the counter with a suddenly cautious aspect, and said with a friendly Western grin,

"Well, you have a good one now, sir."

An Ending

Chester stood outside the Bagel Place waiting for Andrea. It was nearly 2 AM. Now that she owned the restaurant, she stayed until closing time. He would stay with her one last night, and then head back to the mountains. Summer was over and he needed to get back to the mountains before it snowed. He paced along the sidewalk, examining once again the familiar stores. His eyes strayed to the corner, and he found himself walking toward the alleyway. At the corner, he saw a cream-colored Jaguar. It was the same car from the desert, from Las Vegas.

Chester quickened his steps. He entered the alley. The light was meager, but he could see clearly. He could feel the air, the beauty of the early morning dampness, the smells of the street, the stir of a breeze from the ocean, the stray noise from the street. Suddenly he heard the screech of wheels. And then the hi-beamed headlights of the white car. In his eyes. The car barreled toward him and stopped just a foot from his feet. Chester stood transfixed, a steeliness in his limbs and heart. He was ready to die. And ready to live.

The driver's door flew open and Carlos stormed out. He rushed at Chester and seized him by the collar, pushing and lifting him backward. Chester regained his balance, threw out his arm, and chopped Carlos on the Adams apple. Carlos fell to the ground. Chester raised his foot and placed it firmly on Carlos' neck. He hesitated to press his weight forward. He did not want to kill anyone. It just did not sit well with him.

"Carlos, you're a lucky man, Carlos. You're lucky that I'm a phantom, not a normal person. Because a normal person would kill you. You'd be dead. So remember that and go on living anyway. Maybe you could try like working for a living."

As Chester stepped away, Tummie rolled out the driver's door and shot his pistol at Chester. A bullet skipped on the pavement. Chester began to run. There was a large piece of cardboard on the other side of the alleyway. Chester felt a piercing blow to his back, and then the explosion of the gun. Two more shots stabbed him - both entering his chest from the back. One of bullets exited his stomach. He felt its burn, and saw the blood on his shirt. He stumbled toward the cardboard. A form, a shadow of a man, was hovering over it. Chester fell on the cardboard, and was dead. The part of Chester that was a phantom joined the form. And was gone. Into the air.

Another Ending

Chester was up in the mountains. He would always be up in the mountains.

Similarly, he was always down by the ocean.

He had left LA and Las Vegas, and taken up residence in a small town outside Mt. Zion National Park in southern Utah. He worked as a gardener at one of the motels.

The skies were full of glory here. The sun shone deep into the hills and valleys, and slanted across the mountain range that extended westward. Chester stood alone on a large, flat rock, which outcropped a ridge alongside highway 46.

The sun bathed him in warmth and energy. Chester felt he could stand there forever. The rush of the wind was a delight upon him.

Part II
in the continuing saga
of
Chester Knowles

Memories of a Phantom

Editors Note:

The following document was sent to us by Ms. Natale Silver, MSW, a clinical social worker at Las Vegas Medical Center. We make no claims for its authenticity, but publish it here in the hope that it can shed some light on the preceding account of The Lives of Chester Knowles.

Strictly speaking, Ms. Silver's submission is a diary. However, the entries are made by several different persons. It's all in the first person, which may be somewhat original, but, on the whole, it is confusing. We apologize for its rough, unfinished style and its obvious lack of logic. Ms. Silver maintains that this diary was "Chester's last wish." We leave it to the reader to decide whether this document has any merit whatsoever.

Memories of a Phantom

You may ask why I title this book Memories. Had you read the first book about me, which was called *One Life or The Lives of Chester Knowles* (written by the author Stephen Baum) you wouldn't ask be asking. You'd know the how's, whys, and wherefores of my being a phantom, and you'd also know that the *Memories* sections (Baum always italicized the word Memories as if it were something special) were entries in the personal diary of a character named Chester Knowles. And Chester Knowles is *me*. Really. It's me. I am Chester.

You see, I started writing down my memories, as I called them in my little spiral notebook, while I was holed up in a little cabin in the Sierra Nevada Mountains. I was trying to recollect who I was - trying to re-start my life after "dying". It may sound crazy and confusing, and I don't claim to understand too much of it myself, but, what happened was that I had died and somehow been reincarnated in another man's body. It was no easy deal. That's why I am a phantom. So I hope that explains the title.

Let me state right here at the outset that I am a fictional character. Fictional, as in a work of fiction. As in made up, not true. And any resemblance - or semblance of a resemblance - to any person or persons, places, things, dreams, lives, universes, or whatever, in the so-called "real world" is unintentional. Or at least, I didn't mean it. And, even if it were intentional, what are you going to do? Sue a fictional character? Be that as it may, and to return to the matter at hand, i.e., the Memories, I did succeed in the first book, the Lives of Chester Knowles to do one thing: to remember who I was.

I remembered my old life, the life I had forgotten. Don't scoff, don't snicker, don't put it down. It was a big deal for me at the time. All that remembering! It took a long time. Finally, and quite fortuitously, I had the opportunity to re-visit my family in Los Angeles, to help them out a bit, have a bit of fun, meet some very nice women on the way I must add, and even to bring a sort of closure to the personality of my previous incarnation, who was called Tony Santos. I did it. I'm proud of it in a way.

And the book ended well - with yours truly kind of sailing off into the sunset on my astral body, or some jazz like that. I suppose you could call it a spiritually happy ending. Everybody likes a happy ending - especially if it's spiritual, I might add. But I've returned here to try to set the record straight. To clarify, if you will, certain and various misunderstandings.

First of all, there is no such thing as an afterlife. This is a fact. I've been there, done that. There's nothing there. Although, I must say, whatever it is isn't all that bad. It's just a different sort of dimension, or energy, if you will. Actually, the more I think about it, the nicer it seems. But it's like a horse of a different color, an apples and oranges type of comparison. The other world is just very different. Very different. Most definitely, it can't be called living or an "afterlife". Because it's not life! And, as a corollary statement, let me state right now that there is no heaven or hell. Because that's the next question they like to ask you, "Were you in heaven, or did you go to hell?" Well, the answer is neither. None of the above, and none of the below.

I don't know why people hold on to that stuff, that nonsense. Well, it's true that death is frightening at first, and people tend to believe anything that assuages their fears about the matter (or non-matter). The major religions of the world have, of course, a major interest in the death/afterlife business, and they've made quite a pretty penny on it over the millennia. But what I want to tell you is that it just ain't there. If anything, heaven and hell are right here on this earth. In this life, this dumb old life. It's all here.

You have it all: heaven, hell, purgatory, trial by fire, fly by night, cash and carry, soup and salad, and rock and roll. You just need to grab the bull by the horns, make hay while the sun shines, walk on the sunny side of the street (get your coat and grab your hat, leave your troubles on the doorstep)*. And it's all because you only live once. It's just like my mother used to say: "You only live once." My Mom was pretty smart.

So, the question that remains is how to do it right, or most efficaciously. Ethics comes into it, but I would say that the main thing to steer you is aesthetics. I mean "it don't mean a thing if it ain't got that swing". You'll pardon my propensity for the silly quotes, and for the musical metaphors, but there's nothin' like music to reveal the aesthetic. And then there's math, which is the underpinnings, the language, the framework for this whole, stupid, beautiful, call-it-what-you-like world/universe. So let the music play! Let the mathematicians sing!

* Sunny Side of the Street by Dorothy Fields and Jimmy Mc Hugh, 1930

Intro

First I was Chester.

And then I was Tony.
And then I was Chester again.

I stayed with a woman
In the town of Las Vegas.

Her name was Frances.
And here she goes.
Parles-tu, Frances

Frances Speaks

"Musica," I say. Musica! Musica is very important! I can remember quite well that I once told a young man in New York, a young man who loved me - he loved me very much in fact - that his love for music wouldn't last. That he would outgrow it. It was a summer night, after dinner, and we had stopped in our walking in front of a showcase window of a record store on 72nd Street, near Broadway. He pointed excitedly to some records of American folk music. I recall (and I will confess, to be honest, that the next day I returned to check with the salesman at the store) that it was music by a Sonny Terry and a Brownie McGee, two black men from the south. But my young man was so excited, so excited about them, so much the optimist.

I could not bear it of course. I told him coldly, as coldly as I could, which in my case was with a laugh and haughty turn of the head, "Eh, when you are older you won't care about these people so much. You'll see. Your tastes will change."

At first, he did not respond. I had stunned him. But he finally responded that he didn't think his taste or feeling for the music would change when he got older. And I told him, "Yes it would." He himself would change.

Poor boy, he hung down his head like a puppy, saddened by my easy remarks. And he shook his head. Finally he said, "No. I can't imagine myself not liking this music. No, I'm sure that I'll always like this music."

I think of that incident of twenty years ago, because now, when I am older, I see that I myself have lost my feeling for the musica. And I know that it is something terrible. To lose one's feeling for the music is like to lose one's life. I know that now, now that I am an older woman, I am forty already. I don't hide it. Look at me. Look at my breasts! They are still perfect. Achh, my legs! They are so fat. But down to the waist, I am beautiful. I am still attractive. Attractive enough to get by! For I always get by in this life on my looks. I know that I should say that I get by due to my brains (and I am clever enough), but I am also, then, clever enough and honest with myself enough to know that it has always been my looks which have helped me to succeed whatever successes I have achieved in this life.

Chester. We must talk about Chester. I met him at a hotel lobby. The Tropicana. Later I learned that his real name was Willie Miles, but when I met him that first night he told me his name was Chester. And so I always call him Chester. That first night, though, he was a John, like in John Doe, and we went to a room in the Hotel - which was a pleasant gesture on his part. And I became disposed to him. I would often serve him for no money. I am not a complete whore, you know. And, since then... well, we keep in touch. I know where he works, and he knows the places I work, and the manners in which to find me.

I can talk to Chester in a way that I can talk to no man, and certainly to no woman. I can talk the truth to him, and he does not disapprove. He listens to me with such respect. Does he love me? No, he does not love me. But he likes me a bit, and he tolerates all of my bad characteristics. For - now I am facing it - I do have some difficult characteristics. I am, in fact, terrible.

I want too much. Want too much! I am greedy! If it were not for my greediness, I would be happier, so much happier. I covet things. I grasp at them. I want money like a sickness, like a thirst, and I am jealous of other people all the time. And it is because I want things in such an exaggerated way that I will do nearly anything to obtain what I want. And thus it is inevitable that I hurt people very often. And, you know, I am so used to it that it does not bother me any more that I hurt people. I am inured, and made protected from feeling guilt. Because, as I am saying, one just becomes used to it. And finally one just has no guilt anymore, no feelings of guilt. Thus do I possess some power over people at certain times, since I am not burdened with a conscience. But mostly it is unhappiness that I bear and know as a full-time companion. I am so sad that it reaches everywhere for me.

When Chester had heard my story, and been with me, and seen me for what I am, he was sad too. He made me feel that perhaps I need not be so sad. Thus I was encouraged by him. Thus I came to seek him out and value his company.

My name is Frances Villon. Actually, my name is Frecha, which means a flower - in our town in Tunisia where

I was born. When I was a very young girl, aged eight years, we went to France, to Paris - to Belleville, where my parents live to this day. My heart leaps out to my street in Paris. My heart wants to fly to the city of Paris - as well as to my childhood places, where I can still remember the manner in which the sun was reflected on the waters. Always with my people there is a yearning, a restlessness. We long for Jerusalem. We long for Israel. We long for peace. We long for the unity of our people and of ourselves, which would be peace. In such a way, I tend never to forget where I came from. I am always an outsider, for I am aware that I am never in my home. I am like a cat on the prowl. Ehh, I joke.

But I will tell you also that I have stopped longing for a man. I have given up the trying for the finding of a man. This is part of my bitterness, perhaps the main part of it. I no longer care for love. It is too expensive for me, and I am past that. Let it be enough to say right now that I hold Chester dear to me in my heart and wish him no ill - which for me is the closest thing to love that I can manage.

Howard

Hello. My name is Howard Hartman, and Chester is a friend of mine. Unlike Chester, however, my spirit is still in my body. I'm just a regular person, i.e., I'm still alive. Chester told me all about himself and his predicament. But, to tell you the truth, I didn't really understand too much of what he said. It's pretty difficult stuff. But if Chester taught me anything, it's that you only live once. So, if I have a chance to get into this book, to make an entry into Chester's diary, to tell my story too, well then here I am. I realize that I'm taking certain liberties in sneaking into this diary, but what the heck? I see that Frances, who is a good friend of mine, is already in this book, so why not me? In any case, Chester's a good friend of mine too, and I'm sure he won't mind.

I first met Chester in southern Utah, where he was employed at a small motel as a gardener and fix-it man. He was out behind the motel shoveling compost. It was early one Sunday morning that I had slipped out of my room and started on my way down the road. I remember that I noticed him working out back. I don't really recall exactly how it was that I wound up in that motel in Utah. That's the kind of broken-down shape I was in. It's all kind of hazy, that part of my life. A drunken haze.

You see, I had been living and working in Flagstaff, Arizona at the University of Arizona. I was doing my residency in obstetrics. I was in my second year. But that all ended when I broke up with my girlfriend and fiancée, Natale. Actually, it was she who left me, and went to live in

Vegas. Her explanation, her only real explanation, was that I was boring her. I mean, she said a lot of other things too, but the only thing that ever made any sense to me was what she said about my being boring. So after three years of living with me she discovered that she was bored. I don't know, but it shattered me.

I was alone in this world. I had already disowned my parents in Minnesota, and they had disowned me. I am an only child, and, for reasons that are too long to go into, I never had much to do with either of my parents' families. So there I was with no family ties. And my old friends from back home, well, I had left them behind, too. I felt I had nothing left, and it was the God-awful truth. I was alone, and I had nothing. All the while I had been thinking that Natale – my girlfriend, my lover, my everything woman - would save me. I had made my commitment to her. Can you imagine that? To my mind, the very fact that I had made a commitment should have been sufficient to hold her. But it wasn't of course. She was bored with me. That's what she said, and it was the truth. Anyway, she broke up the engagement all of a sudden (just like they do in the movies) and moved to Las Vegas.

I fell into a period of drug and alcohol abuse. Like for about a year. Finally (it took an amazingly long time, now that I look back on it) I lost my job, lost my residency at the hospital, and then I lost my apartment. I began living out of the car. And I was on the road, just drinking, just letting my life go down the drain - when I ran into Chester.

If you can believe it, I was out walking, out on the road, on State Highway 46 in Utah. It was a hazy Sunday morning, already hot, and there I was: out on the road looking for an open bar - somewhere, anywhere to buy a bottle of liquor. Naturally, everything was closed. I was in Utah! I walked back to the motel dry and empty-handed. I had no idea what I was going to do, for, you see, I only lived from minute to minute. But Chester was out back working the compost. He saw me walking back to my room, and he called me over. We got to talking, and before I knew it, I was working for him, shoveling compost. I became his employee, his assistant. And he actually paid me cash at the end of the day - which quite fortuitously covered the motel bill exactly. And I stopped drinking from that day on. Four hundred and twenty four days (I still count, even though Chester says I don't have to).

I learned to go on with my life, to forget about Natale. To start my life again, and to enjoy nature. Chester taught me all that. He also taught me a lot about music. So I am indebted to him in a lot of ways. I also met a lot of cool people through Chester. I gave him a ride back to Las Vegas a couple days later, and that's when I met Willie Miles.

Willie Miles Speaks

Willie Miles is yet another white-haired guy who looks like Chester and also looks like Tony, but who has different-color eyes. Willie dresses more like a cowboy, a country-western singer. As we zoom in on Willie we see that he is hunched over his guitar scribbling words in a notebook. He writes:

> *There been some lonely times*
> *(E to A, like a gospel thing)*
> *E up on the neck, 7ᵗʰ fret. The A- chord is played on the fifth fret with 2 fingers, g string open)*

He speaks in a western twang:

Willie Miles, yes that's my name. I'm a bit busy right now. Sorry 'bout that. It's because we're getting ready to go on for our set. By "we" I mean the band I play with, "The Rangers". We used to be called "The Silver Bullet" and the "Lone Rangers", and we also went by the name "The Lone Rangers and Tonto". Oh yeah. We were also known for a while as "The Tontos", but that was all a long while back.

We do mostly country stuff. Good music, and people like to hear it. Me and the band have established something of an existence here in Las Vegas. Out of thin air, you might say. We play pretty regular in Vegas, though sometimes we travel a bit (a couple of trips to Arizona, a few times to San Diego for gigs, once to LA). Me and the band get along OK. That's band with a small b. Not with a capital B like in the Band. No, we're definitely lower case, and that's important to understand. We're a plain band, and we sometimes make some decent music. Sometimes. I have no more pretensions, no more illusions about this band: it is no longer mine anyway. I just play in it. They still call me Tony. They think that I'm Tony Santos - which, of course, I am, if you give things a bit of a wide sweep. On the other hand, if you take things literally, I am not Tony.

So who's right? Am I Tony Santos? Or am I Chester? Or is it Willie Miles?

Davie Speaks

"Willie Miles it be!" hollered out the bartender Davie, as he made a noisy entrance onto the little stage through a parted red curtain. (That's right, Davie the bartender. What a guy, Davie, waddling out onto the little stage, then calling for Willie to come out.) And out walks Willie, still holding his guitar by the neck. Davie puts his arm around Willie's shoulders, and pulls him close to his body for a moment before letting him go.

"OK, Willie," proclaimed Davie, "Or whoever the hell else yer callin' yerself t'day, let's hear ya play some songs! An' remember ta throw in a couple by Hoagy Carmichael.......(Stage aside) He does them real nice, folks, because I've heard him do these songs several times, on several occasions. He's really good, folks......So let's hear it fer Willie Miles and the Rangers! Everybody!" barked Davie at the crowd, the Saturday evening crowd, which had by now filled most of the tables at this old lounge room - which, like Davie and the rest of downtown Vegas, had seen better times. However, like old times, the lounge room was full.

Enter: the members of the band. The lights in the room dim. Willie turns and walks to his place behind the drums. The band sets up. After only a minute, they're ready to play, and open with a Hank Williams song:

If you loved me half as much as I love you
You wouldn't treat me half as bad as you do.
You know that I would never be so blue
If you only loved me half as much as I love you.

Sitting in the audience, close together, knees touching, are Andrea and Natale - at a front table. Also in the room, also sitting at a front-row table, are Davie and Chester Knowles. Davie has taken his seat and is leaning across the little table and whispering loudly behind the back of his big hand over the noise of the guitar break.

"I don't get it, Chester, how you say you know Willie Miles over there. Oh, I know he calls himself Willie now - instead of Tony, which is how I know him. But, heck, I don't get it how you guys do anything anymore. I guess I'm just an old man that don't know nothin'. But, I tell ya, I like this music him and his band been playin'. Nice simple songs for a change. Nothin fancy. Just real nice. They ain't bad, these kids. They're real nice, yeah. But you shoulda heard them when they first got out here. They wez terrible. Believe me, they wez terrible. But they'ze a lot better now. Real nice, like I'm sayin'." Davie paused to take a deep breath and strike a pensive pose.

"I don't think, though, that it's Vegas that makes them better," continued Davie, finally leaning back in his chair. "I been out here for a good many years...... Say, did I tell ya how many years I been out here, Chester?"

"Thirty?"

"What, ya mean I already told yer? Well, I guess I must be talkin' too much. That's OK. I know I talk too much. But heck, Chester, I like talkin'. Everybody likes ta talk.

"In fact, what I have here is a little preposition ta make, a perposal - although not a perposal of marriage. And definitely not to you, Chester....heh, heh. Anyhoo, what I'm perposin' here is that everybody, all the characters in this here book, get a chance ta talk, to explain themselves, ta tell a story. First person, like. You know, like in the first person? You know, like I, me, mine? I think it'd be real enjoyable,

what with everybody gettin' a chance and all. What do ya say
we give it a try, Chester? For instance, look at Tony up there
- or Willie. Or whatever the heck his name is. He's steppin'
up to the microphone right now. We'll just let him introduce
himself, tell a little about himself, maybe sing a song or two.
He's a real fine singer that Tony".

Willie Miles steps to the microphone

"OK, so you want me to try to introduce myself. OK. Then, it's me, Willie Miles: the Lone Ranger, the next incarnation, the one I had to be. Not everyone gets a second chance, a second chance at life. But I got it. I guess I'm lucky. Some people might get religious, others might get all paranoid, others might just flip out and never come back. Well, I did all of the above. Been there done that. And it looks like I wound up in Las Vegas. I have a friend who's a psychologist who thinks that being in this band and playing the drums and ignoring the rest of life is a bit schizophrenic. Well, I disagree. I just call it good luck. Brains is better than brawn, my mother used to say. But luck is better than brains any day of the week is what I say. And rich or poor it's good to have money. What more can I say than that?

"What we're gonna do right now is to sing a song. Everybody has a story to tell, and it's all the same story. I tell ya, I barely care anymore what the story is. It's just a pleasure to be here and to be able to share some of our music with you. It's just like my friend and guru, Davie Goldstein says: Everybody gets to have a chance. And, this next song is dedicated to you, Davie. It's a song by Hoagy Carmichael and it's called "Georgia On My Mind".*

> *Georgia, Georgia - the whole day through.*
> *Just an old sweet song keeps Georgia On My Mind*
> *Georgia, Georgia - a song of you.*
> *Comes as sweet and clear*
> *As moonlight through the pines.*

Other arms reach out for me.
Other eyes smile tenderly.
Still in peaceful dreams I see
The road leads back to you.

Georgia, Georgia - no peace I find.
Just an old sweet song
Keeps Georgia on my mind.

*Copyright 1930 by Peermusic Ltd. Words by Stuart Gorrell. Music by Hoagy Carmichael.

"Thank you very much," said Willie soberly. He then walked out from behind the drums, picked up his guitar and arpeggioed a full-sounding, open-stringed sort of E chord, and then an open sort of A chord. He methodically went back and forth between the two chords while the other players gradually joined in. Soon, there was a gospel-type rhythm, and the entire room pulsed with excitement. Willie began with the refrain:

There been some lonely times
There been some lonely times

He told his story:

In the darkness of an alleyway
My life did pass before my eyes.
I saw my last chance slip away
I was shot down and I died
Yeah, there been some lonely times
Yeah, there been some lonely times.

But there's no sense in complainin'
The river's chilly and so wide
I spent my whole life in dreamin'
And now there's no place left to hide
Yes, yes. There been some lonely times
Yes, yes. There been some lonely times

So please don't ask me no more questions
I ain't got time to tell no lies
I got a feeling in my heart
Same as the stars up in the skies
Hey, hey. There been some lonely times
Hey, hey. There been some lonely times

So it went. Willie sang lead, and Gene, the bass player, came in on the harmony.

Gene

"OK. My name is Gene. Let me tell you about myself. When I was young, I loved Bob Dylan. I had all his records. I knew all his songs by heart (and I still do). When he went underground, or out of commission, or whatever, in the late sixties, I fastidiously obtained all those underground tapes and records he made with the Band and others. I didn't think much about it at the time. It was just a hobby, and I was this die-hard Dylan fan. But it turned out a couple of years later that my record collection was worth a lot of money - an awful lot. It's been my income. I've pretty much been getting by just by selling off those old tapes to collectors and music companies. They were what were called underground tapes. Well, that whole underground scene is gone today, so it's hard to explain. Today, underground means gritty and hard-edged. But back then there really was some sort of a political underground. Today that's gone, and, like I say, the left wing/underground thing is pretty wasted. So it's just funny that I should have made money out of it. I only mention it because it relates to how I'm gonna introduce myself right now.

I'm Gene, a member of the band. I play bass, and do vocals. And I can play guitar and piano, too. I met Willie Miles back in Detroit, where he used to go by another name, and I played in his band on and off for a number of years. But then I lost track of him, and later he got messed up with some drug stuff. So, I hadn't seen nothin' of him for quite a long period of time. To cut to the windup, the next time I seen him was two, three years later, playin out here in Vegas with this punk band. I jammed with them a couple of times, and then their organist got sick, or he moved back to the Midwest, or somethin like that. Well, pretty quickly it was that I began playin' with Willie, cauz, you see, I remembered Willie as a top-notch player, which he still is, I might add. Just don't let him know that I said that, because I'll never live it down. I tell you, I just like playing music. That's all I'm about.

Anyway, after a while playing together, we started playin' better. And then when Willie made more of a commitment to the band, when he actually started practicing more seriously with the guys, well, then we really started playing good. But we were all a bit confused, because he sounded just like Tony. I mean Willie. He sounds like Tony. And there's people call him Chester. Geez, I got it all gummed up. But that's what I'm trying to explain. I mean it's somethin that you can't explain. Like, there are some things that you can't explain. Why should you even try? You'll just be wastin' your time. At least, that's what I think.

So, to cut to the windup, I think I've succeeded nonetheless in giving you an idea of just how gummed up and confusin' it could be to be playin' with Willie and these guys! And how confusin' the whole thing is altogether. But, as I was also saying, after some time you get used to it. As long as we get to play, I'm all right. And so long as we can make a bit of a living out of it, why, it's a great way to be spendin' some time on planet earth. Because who knows? Perhaps we're all planted here from outer space - sort of like stringed puppets, only we can't see the strings. Like maybe there are aliens, or foreign consciousnesses that put thoughts in our heads, and control us, or use us as vehicles for their own purposes. Like what's the internet, anyway? And, like, what's a soul? The truth is that we don't know. The only thing we do know for certain is that we know nothing for certain.

As I said, my name is Gene. I'm from around Chicago, down near Hammond, Indiana, actually. But I don't want to talk about that. You know, people want to ask you if you knew Michael Jackson etc. It's better when people don't know where you're from. It's better not to get distracted. I mean, the main thing is where we're going. And that's the stars: the nearby planets, and then beyond. The technology is available. I mean for making contact. People just don't want to admit it. I mean, they're discovering new galaxies every day. And out of all those galaxies, there are definitely other people like us out there. People get ready, that's what I say. Get ready. That's about all I have to say for now. People don't like it when I talk about the alien stuff, so I'll just sign off this section of the introductions. In fact (somebody just informed me from back stage), we are, at this point in time, going to be changing the venue for the introductions....... Oh, oh....Hold on a minute.

Sorry.........OK. We are going to California now - sort of like a live broadcast, it'll be an interlude from the diary thing - because we have another couple of introductions to make. Two ladies. Two very nice young ladies, I might mention, so this may be worth your while. And we apologize for the technical difficulties.......

Intro to Andrea and Natale

Yes. It was a beautiful spring day, such as are beautiful in all locales, but are especially beautiful in southern California. The backyard was still in shade; wet avocado leaves lay on the dark grass. The white morning sky could be seen overhead, but the glare of the sun was blocked by a large-spreading rubber tree. Birds chirped, a whippoorwill on the lower branches sung out - as if it were speaking to her personally. A machine, a pump of some sort, hummed in the next yard.

Natale Silver could not believe her good fortune. She smiled broadly, as she leaned on the patio railing. A bird in the tree warbled - as if it was speaking to her. A dog, a large collie, Andrea's dog Candy, stepped out onto the porch and brushed along Natale's leg. She let down her arm to stroke Candy's flank as she passed. Inside, Andrea was singing along to a CD of Bob Dylan's Forever Young, as she washed the breakfast dishes. Andrea and Natale were becoming close friends, each bonding for the first time as a mature woman to another woman. There was a thrill to their new friendship. Both had been lovers of Chester's.

Let us describe them...... Well, were we to cast their parts for the movie version of this book, we might try to get Sandra Bullocks, or, better yet, a young Madeleine Stowe to play Natale. We're looking at a hot-babe social worker/discharge-planner lady here. Natale had studied psychology and clinical social work at the University of Arizona - which is where she met Howard. She met Howard, went out with him for three years, and was about to marry him when.....Well, OK. We know that part already...

Andrea we of course remember from the first book. Andrea could be played by Gwyneth Paltrow perhaps. Andrea was now a successful businesswoman. She had assumed ownership of the Bagel Place two years ago, and had made a few minor changes - primary of which was the purchase of an old, but very good, Italian espresso machine. Business had soared. A neophyte to real estate and investment, she nonetheless took the advice of a customer and purchased this house in West LA, and already had appreciated her equity by half. She had settled into a quiet life, with her mind focused on the business and the house, and, in a change of life-style, she now had few men to disturb her.

But last night, Natale had told her some interesting news of Chester.......

Andrea Makes an Entry in the Memories Diary

OK. I will write in this silly diary of Chester's. Natalie is with me again. I wish I had never met Natale. It's all her fault, in any case, as it was she who pursued me. From the beginning it was she who pursued me, and not the other way around. When she called me up from Vegas two months ago I agreed to meet with her. I was naïve and I thought that she would have information about Chester. But, in actual fact, it was she who was coming to me for the obtaining of information.

I remember our first meeting time very well. She didn't simply come out and just ask about Chester. No, she used her psychologist's tricks. She was sly about it. She took me out to dinner, a very nice dinner. We ate at Gladstone's on the beach, and she treated, she paid. We got along well from the beginning, despite everything. It's always been something special with Natale. A "special relationship", she said. I remember we went for a walk that night along the beach. I remember it so very well: it was the sound of the waves crashing. They were so loud. So powerful, especially at night. It reminded me of things Chester had told me. About how nature is not only beautiful, but powerful and cruel as well. It was as if Chester were there on the beach with us. I swear it.

I remember we held hands with each other because we were both very afraid - standing on the wet sand with all the thunder-noise of the waves. And the cold mist blowing around us. Natale and I immediately became good friends. We have Chester in common, I suppose. So, that night I told her everything about Chester. All of the strange story. The next day she took a plane back to Las Vegas and found him. It was as if she had solved a crossword puzzle. Natale is a practical girl. She became his lover. But with Chester, nothing lasts forever, and he was soon gone from her. Poor girl. Her heart is still broken. She was crazy about Chester. For my own part, I will tell the truth: I was never in love, I was never crazy about Chester. That is to say, I have been crazy over so many men in my short life, that I no longer take myself seriously when I fall in love. Chester says, or said, that I am a master of love. A mistress of love, he corrected himself.

I accept it as a fact that Chester isn't mine. He's not mine to give. He had told me he was leaving in any case. I was not surprised when he left. I never believed any of that nonsense about his being kidnapped. I believed it when I saw Tony dead, however. That's enough for me. Because later, when Tony came back as Chester.....Well, it's not in my ability to understand everything. But I do know that I believe nothing anymore. The skeptic in me has won out. My feet are on the ground, not in the clouds. Natale and all her long tales about Chester cannot move me.

Natale is like my sister. She is. But she does not understand a thing about Chester, poor thing. Too much psychology is a poor influence on a person. Natale believes she understands things when in fact she does not. When they have a name and a category for each and every phenomenon, then they think they understand. But if they understood perhaps a little bit more, then they would see how little they understand in the first place. All the theorizing and building of constructs and systems blinds them and stupefies them - in a likening to a tower of Babel, a tower of confusion. They lose their common sense. Poor

Natale will again try to save Chester. And the funny thing is in that I have agreed to assist her in her nonsense. She says that only when she has resolved all her issues with Chester will she be able to forget him and move on. OK. I will try to help her to try to find her "resolution". Our fates are intertwined in any case. We are bound like sisters.

She is my sister. But yet I wish she hadn't come. Because now I am drawn into Chester's world again. Perhaps it is also not a coincidence that that filthy drug dealer Carlos - who killed Tony in the first place, I am almost certain of it - came into the restaurant two days ago. He told me to take a message to Chester. He wants Chester to come see him, but wouldn't tell me more. I told him I had not seen Chester, which is the truth. He said, "OK. It's cool. Just do it." and he left a one hundred dollar bill on the counter, as if it would buy my confidence. Like that's what I'm worth, a hundred dollars. And he walked out before I could say any response. I still have the hundred dollar bill. Perhaps it is good luck. Or perhaps bad luck. Everything was good for me, things were quiet and peaceful for me. But now I will have to enter into Chester's wonderful, but very crazy, world.

Chester and Andrea Interlude

On one hand I count the reasons I should stay with you
To have you close to me all night long.
So many lovers 'games I could play with you.
On that hand there's no reason why it's wrong.
*But on (*and here we have a dramatic chord change
into the fourth*) the other hand*
There's a golden band.
To remind me of someone who would not understand.
On one hand I could stay and be your lover man
*But the reason I must go is on the other hand. **

*On the Other Hand, D. Schlitz and P. Overstreet, ASCAP
1986

Chester sung along with the Randy Travis CD in his
boom box, which sat on the walkway of the motel. Chester
had lined up all his wrenches on the gravel. He spilled out a
coffee can of bolts and odd pieces, for he needed to fashion
an odd fitting to repair the plumbing in one of the rooms.
There was no rush. He had all day. He could do whatever he
liked with the tools and construction materials his boss Pat
kept in the work shed. Pat had given Chester "carte blanch".
Chester now spent nearly all his time at the motel tending to
the garden, doing repairs. Ruth and Pat, the owners, loved
him. They were glad to leave all the maintenance work to
Chester, and he could be trusted.

Chester occasionally went into Vegas to work with the band, but mostly the band was on its own. Gene had taken over much of the singing and arranging. Still, Chester was always working on new material. They'd have to do this Randy Travis song when he got to Vegas. He loved to play country-western songs. When he was younger, he looked down disparagingly at "country-western". He favored folk music and jazz, and later on rock music. The old country songs were great, but not the whiney, commercial, country-western stuff. He used to find it offensive when he was Chester Knowles. But now he liked it. He loved singing and playing country songs. He didn't care whether he was Tony, or Willie Miles, or even himself.

He was well satisfied with this easy life - shuttling between Las Vegas and southern Utah. He didn't mind that he wasn't accomplishing anything. He didn't worry whether or not he was creating great art. His only sorrow was the loss of his family. It was a pain that fueled him. A pain he carried in his chest wherever he went. The occasional visits as Uncle Willie were, in some ways, worse than not seeing them at all. Willie would remain faithful to them, but the visiting was not a solution. He would have to learn to live without them. They were all right. They had plenty of money, thanks to the life insurance and lawsuit, i.e. his death. He didn't have to do anything: just to stay out of the way. It was a bitter lesson, but he had to accept it, even savor it.

He returned to his plumbing work. Employing an old piece of plastic he had found on the road, he filed and sanded until it served as adaptor to connect the tubing. Chester stood back to regard his tools and his work. The sidewalk was a clutter, but the pipe fitting stood out as a masterpiece. He was eager to try it on the plumbing.

Andrea drove up in a dusty Toyota Corolla, and Chester could see it was her even before she parked the car at the motel entrance. She saw him too, immediately. She left the car door open; she ran to his arms. "Oh, you Chester. I am so glad you are OK?" She kissed him repeatedly.

Their embrace was long. She finally pushed him back a bit with her thigh, smiling and repeating "Ooh, you Chester!"

Chester returned his plumbing tools to the metal toolbox, and collected all the odd pieces. He carefully placed the plastic piece in a small paper bag. He returned everything to his tool shed, and then washed up outside, using the garden hose. He helped Andrea bring in her suitcase. Without a word they stumbled into Chester's room, and landed on the bed. They made love until suppertime.

Chester prepared rice noodles - with a vegetable sauce he cooked up in a Chinese wok. They drank green tea, which he had grown alongside the motel driveway. He let her talk. She told him about Natale. She told him of her visit from Carlos, and she gave him a crumpled hundred dollar bill, which Chester quietly took and promised to deliver. He said he would take care of it. Then she told him how well things had gone for her: her successes at the store, her new house, her sense of being herself and not someone else.

"So, is it time to go back to Amsterdam?"

"Acch, Chester. You just say things for no reason. I do not know how you do it, but you always touch me. You are right, of course. I am thinking about it. Not all of the time, but I am thinking about it. But it is not the correct time yet. When it is time, I will know. I tell you, Chester, I am really all right."

"So how long can you stay here? A month? A year? You can bring your dog, too!" he proclaimed, as he kissed her. "I love having you. I've always loved you, you know that.... Say, there's someone you have to meet. A guy in the band. His name is Willie Miles. He's actually a part of me, or a part of my spirit, and he's also part Tony. Tony is the one he's really like........"

"Acch, there you go again, you Chester, with your silliness. You are a very silly man, for a grown man. And so you see it is only because I love you so much that I can forgive how silly you have become. That is a sign of how much I love you. An indication."

"Andrea, could you give me an indication of how much of an indication you're talking about?"

"Ooof, Chester. Listen to me. It is because of Natale that I am here. You see, she is in love with you. Or rather, she is in love with Willie. Aachh, what does it matter? What is important is that she loves someone who is not really there. I know you have told me about yourself so many times. And Chester, after all of these explications, I remain in the dark. I cannot see. I do not know what is real and what is not. You are a phantom, just as you say…. Chester, you know that I love you. However I do not love you in the way that I would love a normal person. But Natale, she does not know the difference. You have to help her. She needs to move on with her life. She thinks, furthermore, that she needs to save you: that you need saving. Hah! While it is she who requires the saving! So, what I am trying to tell you, you silly man…..oof….. Put your hands down… Wait a bit. Chester, you must promise me, you will help her. She is crazy for you, which is the same thing as to say she is crazy with a period….Ooof …. Chester, stop…."

Howard's Memories

Hi. It's me again, sneaking into this diary book. Again, I don't think Chester would mind. My name, by the way, is Howard Hartman, just to remind you, and I'm here to tell you my story - which, it turns out, is also part of the Chester story, the Tony and Willie story, as well as everyone else's story. I mean, it all comes together. Trust me.

I first came up to Vegas together with Chester. I gave him a ride. Chester never had a car, although I think he had enough money for one. You see, even though I'd been traveling all around Arizona, I'd never been to Vegas before. It was quite a shock, because Vegas is quite a weird place. But after a spell, I got used to it, and even though I can't say I like it, I can say that I'm used to it. Isn't that what they say about New York City? I don't know, because I haven't been around that much. Just Minnesota and Arizona. Both of those places have enough of everything to keep you satisfied, or at least they should. People are always talking about different places, but it doesn't matter much to me. There's beauty everywhere, although some places are somewhat easier. I will say that.

As I was saying, I drove Chester to Las Vegas, and, believe it or not, who should I run into first thing? ... Natale - the woman who had ruined my life, or rather, the woman who I thought had ruined my life, or who I had allowed to ruin my life. Whatever. You see, I had driven Chester back to Vegas because Chester was playing drums and guitar in this rock&roll/country&western band. I wound up playing with them almost immediately. It was a lot of fun to start playing guitar again, especially because I never had played with anyone so good before. I just fell right into it. In fact, I'm still into it. Playing with the band on a pretty regular basis. Chester dropped out, or at least most of the time he's out. I usually fill in for him. And the younger guys, as well as Willie and Gene aren't the most dependable either, so you have to fill in a lot. It's just that kind of band. Sort of like interchangeable pieces, which Chester says is superior, although I forget why.

Anyhow, they all play pretty good, and we all like it. That's the main thing. So, as I was saying, I was having a lot of fun up there with Chester and his friends - up there on the stage. We were playing this big lounge room, when in walks Natale. She acted surprised at first to see me, but then she turned hard, like I seen her do a thousand times, and said, with her big wide smile, "What's up?" or somethin like that.

Well, I lost my concentration for a minute. I didn't know whether I was happy or sad, or angry, or loving. Or what. Sort of like I couldn't decide which to be? And so I remained suspended and silent? Chester taught me that, by the way. He said that when you don't know what to do, don't do anything, just watch.

Natale softened and smiled warmly at me, and right then and there I realized that I didn't care about her anymore. Well, not that I didn't care. I still cared. I loved her. And I always will. But I wasn't crazy about her anymore. I could just as easily walk away. The realization of my indifference was very powerful. Camus calls it the "benign indifference of the universe". Well, for me, being indifferent to Natale was so benign that I just stood there with nothing to say. I was just enjoying it. I watched her go and sit down with her friends. And after the set was over, we had drinks at their table. Chester introduced me to everyone.

He made like he was the MC - you know, like he was still onstage - and he introduced me around the table. Chester can actually be quite charming and funny, though most of the time with me he's very serious.

"OK, Howard," he announced, "these are all very special people at this table, so let's give them each their proper respect and attention. I want you to pay attention here, Howard." Chester nudged me in the ribs.

"Let me introduce you, first of all, to you Andrea. She is my friend from Los Angeles. A very good friend of mine. And then there's Davie.... Davie, I want you to be nice to this young fella. OK, Dave? No body slams. OK, Davie?......Now let's see.... Yeah, Howard. I want you to meet Natale, a friend of ours, as they say. You know Natale, right?"

Again, I didn't answer. I just stood there. Chester had already made me pretty smart. Because I'm naturally quite stupid. I admit that. That's another one of the things Chester taught me: that I'm stupid. And I guess knowing how stupid I am ought to make me smarter. But no. I'm so damn stupid that even when I get smart, I'm still pretty stupid. Is that stupid, or what?

Natale and I finally got to talking. We went outside for a walk. It was chilly. In the fall, it gets surprisingly cold in Las Vegas at night. Right off, she began to explain to me how "concerned" and "guilty", and "involved" and "connected", she felt toward me. I use quotation marks, because she said these words like she was reading them out of a book. You have to understand that I'd been out of the university and out of the intellectual circles for quite a time by then, so all those Psych 101 words sounded like a load of BS to me - and they still do, matter of fact. I think it was when she used the word "connected" for the third or fourth time, that I told her, "Listen, Natale. What you're saying is all right, but there's a lot of water that's passed under the bridge. It's like Bob Dylan said: 'Don't think twice, it's all right'."

At that she gave me a big hug and told me that we'd always be friends, "just friends". She used those exact words. She hugged me for a long time in order to communicate her "concern". Well, I guess Natale is a beautiful woman, and before I knew it, I was getting aroused, and I had to turn myself away from her just so she wouldn't notice and get the wrong idea. But when I did that, she thought that I was going through some "difficult passages". But actually, like I said, it was just a boner. But Natale, great psychologist that she is, thought I was "obsessed". Well, what could I do? I knew that I'd only put my foot in it - and Natale would pounce on all my Freudian slips - so I just kept quiet for a while, and let her do all the talking. She went on for quite a while about her responsibilities at the hospital in Las Vegas, and how she maintains a "professional distance".

Well, one thing I did learn about psychology from Natale is that when a person says one thing they usually mean another. Putting two and two together isn't that hard. They call that analysis. Bottom line was that Natale was interested in old Chester. Romantically interested. Which was fine with me, except for that she wanted me to tell her his address in Utah, which I thought was a bit out of line. After all, if she was so concerned - and all those other words - with me, how could she ask me to fix her up with Chester? I thought it was bad taste on her part, but I didn't tell her that. I didn't say anything. I just looked down the street - at the streetlights, the cars out on the Strip. And then Natale began to cry. I mean, really cry. And then I realized how lucky I was not to have married her. What I told her to stop her from crying was that things have a way of working out for the best, even if we can't always understand it. And I then took a page from her book and told her that she and I had reached a certain "closure".

She immediately stopped crying, looked at me hard in the eyes, and asked,

"Howard, do you mean that? Do you really think we've reached closure?"

I said, "Oh yeah. Definitely closure."

Natale broke into tears again. We fell into an embrace again, but this time it was a "just friends" type of embrace. In other words, I didn't get a hard-on. Luckily. And Natale and I have remained "just friends" ever since. It's cool. I think Chester had another little fling with her, though. They'd known each other for quite a time, I believe. And, I believe, it was more than just a little fling. It was a big flingeroo, at least for Natale it was. I swear, Chester threw that lady for a loop and a half, which gives me a kind of pay-back somehow.

You see, with Chester all the romance and the falling in love stuff are like water off a duck's back. Everything's like some kind of natural, animal process with Chester, and he never gets too crazy or worked up about anything. Chester just enjoys himself. He's there and then again, he isn't there. That's another thing he tried to teach me, but which I don't understand very well: how to stay on the outside at the same time you're really on the inside. Perhaps it's vice versa. Staying on the inside, while you're really on the outside. Inside, outside, whatever. I have trouble remembering Chester's words exactly.

I do remember that night very well, though. It was a wonderful night. We went back on stage to play our final set, and it was mostly a country set, which is unusual for us, because we usually like to finish with our rock stuff. I remember Chester sung a Randy Travis song that I used to know, "On the Other Hand", which I love doing the slide guitar part on. And we also did a lot of Hank Williams - well, we nearly always do a couple of Hank Williams songs. Everybody likes Hank Williams. It always goes over well. I remember we finished with "Jumbalaya". Anyway, after the show, Natale just kind of disappeared. She wasn't at the table, and I admit I was kind of relieved. I think she went off with Andrea, or maybe it was Chester. I was just standing around with Gene and Davie after the set - when up walks Frances. I'd met Frances a couple of nights before, which is only natural because she's a friend of Chester's. Frances is a prostitute. I didn't know that at first, although it seems everybody else did. In any case, it's a fact that Frances is a prostitute. She kind of presented herself to me, and it was like in a dream, because off we went for the night - back to my room at the motel, which was only down the block. And I must say, it was quite a night. A night of fantasy, of dreams come true. And I have a confession to make. I fell in love with Frances that night. Hook, line, and sinker. Head over heels. Frances changed my life. Even before we had sex, she said to me that she could tell that I was the "kind of boy who had too many dreams in his head".

She said that she had the capability - the capacitée is the word she used - to bring me down to earth. "I'm going to make you feel the earth." I know she speaks a bit clumsily. Frances is from France, and she has a strong accent, as well as a European perspective on things. So when she said that she'd make me "feel the earth", she didn't mean it literally. After all, she's a hooker, and she was hustling me. And, in that respect, she knew just what to say. But to me it was literal. I wanted to feel the earth in a literal sense. Frances said that she knew life well because she had been down so long. She said that she was like the dregs of some coffee filter. Life had just gone through her. She had had a hard life and she had been down. But it was more than that, because I had been down too.

Actually all my life I had been down. I'd been down so long that I didn't even know it anymore. I had been living in illusions. But Frances showed me reality.

Natale's Memories

OK, it's my turn, finally. Chester said it's OK if I write in this book. It's right here on his table, and he's given me permission. And I must say that I feel privileged – well actually, in a strange sort of way, I feel "entitled" to write in this book. (I never thought I would use that word) After all, when Chester was in the hospital, I was the one who recovered this Memories book in the first place. I remember when I brought it into his room, Chester rose up out of bed like Lazarus from the crypt. The book was in Chester's dirty, beat-up old backpack, which I had obtained for him from the lost articles room in the basement - something which is definitely not in my job description. In fact everything I did for Chester was out of my job description. I must point out - and I know I'm being narcissistic - that Chester has never, at any time, ever expressed any gratitude to me. It's something that I feel very cheated about, even though I know I shouldn't.

But it was I who got Chester back on his feet. I got him out of the hospital. If it weren't for me, he might still be there. The head nurse and my supervisor wanted to place Chester on a 72 hour hold, but I got him signed out surreptitiously. Actually, I did that more than once for patients that I liked or felt sorry for. But then a few weeks later I actually went to check up on Chester - which was also on my own initiative and time. I found him living with these dreadful, pimply, pothead, musician types. It was I who made the connection with him; I threw him a lifeline. I was Chester's link to reality. I know I shouldn't be tooting my own horn like this, but what the hell, it's true. I provided what is called a nurturing relationship. I took care of him. Chester's like a baby after all. He still is. I remember we drove up to Utah, and he said that he would like to live near St. George, and he pointed out a few places he liked. Sort of like a real estate agent would discuss properties. Well, he wound up staying there. So, when he disappeared from my life, I knew where to find him. It was only his exact address that I lacked. Also it was I who put him back in touch with Andrea, and Andrea is good for him. I'm not jealous, though. I'm not angry. I don't regret anything. I've worked this all through - on my own.

My analyst doesn't understand why I'm not more totally furious with Chester, like why I should put up with all his shit. She asks: "Where's the commitment? Where's the commitment?" I know she's right, and I have a lot of work to do on why I just accept things so easily sometimes. But Chester is a take-it-or-leave-it proposition. And if I had wanted commitment, I could have had commitment with Howard. Howard was ready to jump off a cliff for me. And in some respects he kind of did, and I still feel a bit guilty about that. If I wanted commitment, I could have had Howard, like I say. In fact I could even have Howard now. But all I want is Chester, goddammit. Chester.

And even though he isn't here to read this, I'm writing it down in his "personal diary". All the same, though, even if did he read it, he wouldn't care. Chester doesn't give a shit about anything. In fact he's disappeared again. Just vanished. Just like he always does. Andrea's told me some stories about Chester's vanishing that are really bizarre (but which would clearly be a betrayal of our confidentiality for me to mention here). Let me tell you, though, they're pretty damned weird, - even if only half of them are true - or even half true. Admittedly, Andrea is a poor historian, she is a bit borderline. The point here is that Chester is a master at disappearing, and then reappearing. It's his M.O.

Chester wears personalities like suits of clothes, or hats. Chester's like a magician. He'll be back. He always is, the bastard. And I suppose that I will remain very conflicted and very angry. But the bottom line is that I love the bastard. Chester I love you! And you don't love me. But I love you anyway! There, I've said it. And I hope you read this and feel guilty for five minutes at least.

Willie Steps Up to the Plate

That's me, Willie. The Say Hey Kid, Willie Miles. Everyone probably forgot about me. After all, Chester seems to have forgotten about me. He's lost his personality. He's forgotten who he was. He says he's just a phantom, and if you question that, then he'll say that he's just a fictional character. Well, I guess he is. And who am I to criticize? After all, I'm just another part of Chester. And how can the pot call the kettle black? But they say there's no such thing as a free lunch. And it's me who's picking up the tab for Chester and all his shenanigans. I'm talking about his family. Laurie and Vicki. And his wife, Marsha. Chester says they're doing fine, that they don't need him anymore, that they need to grow without him. That they don't need no interference. He compares them to trees that need to grow in a natural, free way. I suppose he's right about that.

It's for sure that the girls are growing wonderfully. Every time I see them, my heart swells with happiness. They're getting big now. Laurie is nine and Vicki is twelve. They're beautiful, but quiet, girls. Particularly Vicki, she's quiet and withdrawn, a lot like Chester. She sits and thinks when she's alone. And she seeks out solitude. Some people need that. Marsha didn't understand that at first, but she sees it now. The only problem for today's kids is that there's so little quiet in the world. They're always plugged into something. There's always something "on". And the music and TV, as well as the internet stuff, is very harsh, too stimulating.

And it's mostly based on fear. That's why everyone you meet is so nervous and stressed out. Too much electricity. Too mush noise. Gene says that microwaves and other radiations infect our nerve cells and cause cancer. Gene's half crazy, but there's something to what he says. People need a chance to be quiet. They need it on a physical level. That's why Chester is always up in the mountains. Well, not always.

Last week I took the bus with Chester to LA. I went to see the family, but Chester didn't. That's what I'm talking about. Chester is on some sort of mission. I tell you, he's crazy. He seems to think that the job he has to do for that punk Carlos is more important than his family. Chester's probably going to get killed, and he seems to accept that. He has no problem with that. But me, I have a problem with that. I don't know. I like living. I like our family. I like the band and the music. I know I act like some hippie musician when I'm up in Vegas, but inside of me, I'm just the same old Chester I used to be. Only now, I need to play Willie, too. You know, the Lone Ranger.

So when we pulled into LA. Chester goes straight to this strip bar. That's where we parted. He's on his "mission": trying to rehabilitate drug dealers and gang bangers or something like that. I tell you, I'm fed up with Chester. So I've let him go. Let him go. For me, everything is still Marsha and the girls. How can I tell you how much I love Marsha? The fact that I try to keep a distance from her only makes me love her more. When she suffers, I suffer too. Without thinking, without knowing, I feel it. I feel it for the girls too. So, I need to maintain a distance from them. I need to let them go. I know that. I need to let them grow on their own. So it's hard. Because I love them so much. And I can't really express myself. I tell you, it's hard. It's hard, but yet it's so beautiful.

Davie

OK, it's my turn now, and let me tell you, I can tell you some stories that can put your hair on end! Me, myself, I ain't got no hair. I lost it all during the war. I've been bald - like a cue ball, heh, heh - for a good many years. A lot of the guys in the Pacific lost their hair too, so I ain't so special. I also lost three brothers in the war, all within one week they got shot down. We was all in the Air Force.... OK, I lost my wife, Esther, ten years ago, and I still miss her something terrible. We never had no children, because Esther had women's trouble, so we never got to have any children. I'm not complaining about that. I'm just explaining that I'm pretty much all alone. It's been a good life so far, though. I've had a lot of losses, as they say, but still - and this is what I want to tell you, to put down in writing - I feel like I have everything. The whole world is mine. I'm on top of the world and my feet are hanging down. That's a line from an old blues song called "Sitting on Top of the World", or something like that.

Chester taught it to me. My memory isn't what it used to be. When you get to be my age these things start happening to you, and you either accept it, or you drive yourself crazy.

People ask me how come I accept things so easy. I tell them that you simply have no choice. Whatever God dishes out, I put on my plate - and eat it! Maybe that's why I'm such a husky guy. It is true that I'm a bit overweight, but what the hell. Am I supposed to stop eating?

I been tending bar for nearly sixty years. I'm 82 now, and I started when I got out of the service. Actually I was working in bars long before then, as my older brother, Harry, may he rest in peace, worked with the bootleggers back in Chicago, and he got all of us kids - there were five of us in the family - he got us all jobs working in bars, even though we was little and underage. I used to clean up in a bar called the Green Emerald, which was a well-known establishment back then. You wouldn't think it was any decent kind of place for a twelve year old kid to be hanging out, because there was a whorehouse, a brothel, right upstairs. But I never seen how it done me any harm. We all turned out OK, me and my brothers, they should rest in peace. I'm the only one left. The last of the Moheegans.

It was a tough place to grow up, Chicago, back in those days. You had to fight, or at least be ready to fight, all the time. I was a big kid even back then, so I learned to take care of myself and my brothers. I'm eighty-two years old now, and I still don't take no shit. I guess I could have done with a little more education. Heck, I barely ever went to school. I had to work and make money for my Mom. We would all bring all our money, every penny of it, home to my mother, God bless her, may she rest in peace. My mother was a wonderful woman. Anywaze, I never been too strong on reading and writing. But, heck, I know what's what. And that's a lot more than you could say for a lot of these professors and doctors that go walking around. They say that I'm distlexic, or somethin' like that. Which means I can't read or write too well - which I could have told you right away without the fancy medical words. The windup is that I get by. I watch the news on TV. I don't watch none of them shows. Them shows are too stupid even for a distlexic guy like myself. And I listen to the radio, too. It's like I been sayin', I know what's what.

But Chester and Willie Miles, and Tony too - that whole business is somethin' I don't understand. The first time I met Tony was a few years back, out here in Vegas, and we made a couple of dollars together. And then I heard he got himself shot, which I felt kind of poorly about, because I was involved and implicated in the whole business he was into. And then, one fine day, out of the blue, in he comes – walkin' into my bar like nothin' ever happened. And he says his name is Willie Miles, and now I even hear people callin' him Chester, which is what I sometimes call him myself.

I mean, back in Chicago everybody had a nickname, and there were aliases too. AKA's and the like. But I never seen anything like this, because this is like people coming back from the dead. What it comes down to is that individual people don't matter. Don't make no difference. Everybody is kind of like the continuation of somethin' else. It all fits together like the pieces of a jig-saw puzzle. Except, only God gets to see the whole picture. We human beans only get glimpses. Willie's friend Howard, was tellin' me the other day that everybody - all of God's creatures - are made of basically the same chemicals or atoms.

Now Howard is a pretty educated fella. He was almost a doctor, an MD. But he's real stupid when it comes to most practical things. Talk about knowin' what's what! Howard don't know "you know what from shinola." Well, he knows, but it comes to him harder than most people. Like me, for instance. I knew what was what when I wez ten years old. I wez sweepin' floors, an' I knew what's what. Anywaze, Howard says that we all come from the sun, and that we're all made of the same stuff, the same type of molecools or somethin' - even the insects and bugs, and the dinosaurs and the monkeys in the jungle, and even the plants, and trees, and cows and whatnot. We're all the same. So, as I wez sayin', you wouldn't expect a damn cow to understand all the pieces of God's plan. Or a moose, or a coconut tree. So why should a person, who's also made of the same stuff, even begin to think that he can understand anything?

Anyway, we can't. What I'm sayin' is that it's only a stupid person who thinks that he's smart. We have to know our place. And Willie and Chester, they know their place. And who am I to judge, anywaze?

Frieze-Frame: Chester Sums It Up

OK. There you have it. That's my diary. Call it The Memoirs of an Amnesiac. Hah! Or The Memories of a Phantom, or More in the Life and Lives of Chester. Call it what you will. It doesn't matter. What does matter, you ask? Go find out for yourself! I'm not telling! Just because I'm a phantom and have sidestepped death a couple of times doesn't make me an expert. Everybody has to find these things out for themselves anyway. You can't be lazy. Me? Well, I've just been lucky. The point, if you insist on there being a point, is that it's good to be lucky. It always helps. And you can take that wisdom and that good fortune - and along with a dollar and fifty cents - you can get on the bus.

Looking back, I surely cannot complain. I had it made in the shade for a while. It was like heaven on earth, if you'll excuse the expression. I played music, I hiked in the mountains. I had a quiet corner and some peace and quiet. I had friends. My wife and children were doing fine back home, in LA. They had forgotten me, and by me I mean Chester, Chester Knowles. I figured it was better to let Marsha stand on her own, and really she's been doing wonderfully, and the girls are growing nicely. Marsha collected over three million dollars insurance money from the malpractice suit, so financially they are set. I felt, and I still feel, that they are better off without me, that they need to live their lives, and grow without me or Uncle Will always poking around. They still mourn for me, Chester Knowles, which is touching, but obviously unnecessary. Even if I were really dead, conventionally dead, there would still be no need to mourn. I had a good life, and there's nothing to feel bad about. I still send gifts to the girls, but they don't know where I am. Once you've lost all that personality stuff, it's easy to see that you're not needed all the time. Life goes on and all of that.

Here in Vegas, I was needed for a while to set up the band (Now, this part is the hardest to explain). I've already told you that Tony was dead, and his personality was also dead - even though I was walking around with his body. But his desire to play music was something so strong and sweet that it could not be denied. Well, maybe I could have resisted it, but what the hell. It was a gesture on my part to Tony's soul that he be allowed to play out his dream. It was a favor, a gesture that I did for him.

And I love the music too. It's something beautiful, and things of beauty don't die. The extension of beauty into time, as well as other dimensions, is something that I learned, too. It sort of defines the word beauty. Beauty is that which is able to extend, or jump dimensions....OK, I'll stop. I know. I retain that trait from Chester's personality: the need to try to explain everything. On the other hand, the obsession for explanations has produced modern technology and the skyscrapers of the modern age. OK, point granted, the modern world is no great prize, but all the same you have to admit it's quite a noble venture. The urge to explain everything is in itself something beautiful. It's a thing of beauty too. That's what I'm trying to say, albeit in self-defense. Abstracting is a beautiful activity. It persists in time, and it persists in me.

The ways of the world, its laws and patterns, remain an immense and beautiful puzzlement.

Howard Sets Things Straight

Well, that's where Chester's diary ended. April 21, 1998. He stopped writing after that. Chester disappeared a couple of days after that, probably on April 23rd. It's been a few weeks now. He is gone. Apparently it's not the first time it's happened. Andrea says he's disappeared several times in the past, and not to worry. But all of us have been deeply affected. Someone said that we shouldn't worry so much, that after all we're just a bunch of fictional characters, as is Chester. But let's get real. Chester is simply very important to us all. We just never realized how important he was until he was gone. And, like I said, he's just disappeared.

Frances takes it philosophically. She says she saw Chester through a car or taxicab window the same day he was kidnapped. From the way she tells it, she saw him at the precise moment he was being kidnapped. She insists that he said goodbye to her, and that he will not be coming back.

Andrea, Chester's old girl friend, who I saw last week in LA, says that Chester will be back, but that she doesn't know when. Andrea owns a little restaurant in L.A., and Natale took me there to tell Andrea the details about Chester's disappearance. Actually, I don't know exactly why it was she dragged me to L.A.

When we got there and finally talked to Andrea in this little coffee shop that she has, Andrea just shrugged her shoulders and said something in Dutch. She was amazingly nonchalant about it, and insisted that we shouldn't worry. Natale, however, is going nuts, absolutely bonkers. Chester's disappearance is "the roughest separation of her life", she says, which is kind of a weird thing to be telling me, I think. Anyway, she spends hours on the phone and on the internet. She talks with the police, as well as certain hospital workers, and various social and law-enforcement agencies in Vegas that she knows. Gene is also running around like a nut. He and Natale have teamed up to form a "crazy squad". That's what we call them.

There are a lot of questions to be answered, but Chester taught me to always start with the hardest question first. And that is this: How come, if Chester and Willie were one and the same person, that Willie is still playing in the band? Willie is still around! And Willie said that I should just shut up and concentrate on my playing. Willie is not worried about Chester at all. The question is: how could Chester have separated from Willie? Unless Willie is just some astral body, or a figment of our imagination, Wilie should be one and the same with Chester. Apparently he isn't. The fact that Willie is a fictional character doesn't explain anything either. It's no excuse and it's not an explanation either.

I'll be honest here and confess that I don't know why my feathers are so rustled about this identity thing. After all, it's no big deal. I ought to just accept it and move on. I suppose it's my upbringing, my education. You see, I didn't have much of a childhood, what with my parents both being such schizoid, anti-social alcoholics and all. Alcoholics are supposed to be gregarious. But no, my folks were isolationists. And drunkards to boot. They didn't have much time for little Howard. Not much nurturing. There weren't any other family members to care for me, either. All I had was books. Books were my entire life.

I read science mostly, and I studied medicine. And my belief was in science, which meant that everything must have an explanation. Actually, today's science is sophisticated enough to see that any phenomenon, when closely examined, is quite mysterious. Like the web of a spider, for instance. Or the structure of a molecule. It's all quite indeterminate, and mostly space - so large as to overwhelm our tiny, little, barely-evolved, mammalian brains. So, why can't I just accept things? Why should knowing where Chester went and where Willie began matter so much to me? Why can't I just "shut up and listen to the music"? - which is what Willie said to do.

Natale says that I'll have to "work it all through". She's working it all through herself, although it looks like she's just putting herself through another wringer. She believes in psychotherapy the way most people believe in Jesus Christ. She spends all her money on therapists, and they just take her for a ride. Her latest therapist told her that she should get back with me, or at least to "explore" it. I don't think I care to be explored, even by Natale. I think the whole therapy game is pretty weak, which means I should be giving up on the scientific, rational explanations as well. But, to quote Natale, I guess I'll have to "do some more work" on that.

Anyway, I'm going to leave some space for Willie to write, although I'm not promising it'll make sense. Making any sense is against Willie's religious principles.

Willie Takes Another Turn at It

Howard insists I write something. I'm no writer. I'm a musician. It's in my blood. It was in Tony's blood, by way of his grandmother, and it's in me. It's the part of me of which I am totally sure. But that's neither here nor there. The question everyone's asking is whether I am really Willie Miles? Of course I am. Am I Chester Knowles? Of course not. My name is Willie Miles, and I have a social security card, a driver's license, and also a credit card, as well as membership in the Musician's Union. I am piece of the spirit the same way you or anybody else is. We're all just pieces of the spirit. That's my religious principle, the extent of my thinking on the matter, or should I say non-matter?

Chester likes to analyze and classify things, and poor Howard, our lead guitarist, is similarly afflicted. In fact, Howard is such a jumbled mess, such a tangle of thoughts and opinions, that his poor over-worked brain might never calm down. Because my feeling is that we're all just pieces of the spirit, pieces of the energy of this world. And that if you contemplate on that, then it ought to be enough. Sorry if I don't illuminate what's happening, but I never made any promises to that effect. It was Howard who led you down that path, and I make no excuses for him.

What happened to Chester was this (and don't ask me how I know, because I ain't tellin'). Chester was walking down Las Vegas Blvd. Chester walks everywhere. He says it's healthier, and he always makes a big deal of physical exercise and the great outdoors. That's why he spends most of his time up in the mountains. Anyway, he was walking up the Strip when someone called to him from a white Jaguar. Chester went over and got in the car. He wasn't kidnapped - like everyone thinks. He wasn't abducted and shanghaied like the first time. No. Chester opened the door and got into the car himself. On and of his own accord and volition. Chester knows what he's doing. Chester may be stupid, but he's not dumb. He's back in LA right now. I went there together with him on the bus. Right after he spoke to Carlos and those guys, that's when we left. We took the bus, and we parted in Hollywood. But I'm not sure if and when he'll be returning to Vegas. Chester doesn't know himself. That's it. Chester's still in LA.

Frances Parle Encore

Let me tell you about something about Chester before we continue. I need to tell this to someone. Because yesterday I received a visit from his friend Gene, and Gene told me how Chester is missing, and did I know anything. Etc, etc, and so forth. Well, I was honest when I told him that I hadn't heard from Chester in several weeks. However, I did not tell all that I knew. I felt bad about this later, although I admit I did not feel bad at the time. But I am accustomed to not speaking directly. Gene should have asked further questionings. It's not my fault that he didn't ask correctly. But perhaps, though, now that I think in a more rational manner, I should have simply told Gene the truth. Gene is a good friend of Chester's and is quite harmless in any case.

Well, the truth is that I had seen Chester off the Strip only several weeks before. It was on a Sunday night, and he was in the back seat of a big white Jaguar. They were pulling out of the driveway of that fancy condominium over there. Well, I saw him. He saw me too and motioned to me with a kiss - a farewell kiss. I am sure that is how he meant it, for he puckered his lips and looked at me. It was a loving look. A farewell. A parting look. I am sure of it. I have said goodbye to dozens and dozens of men in my life, and this was one of those goodbye looks, a kiss blown to me through the closed window of a passing automobile, a Jaguar.

I will tell you the truth now. My primary feeling is not one of sadness. Rather my first impression and sentiment - the one that remains strongest to me - was that

Chester flattered me. He loved me and he blew me a goodbye kiss. He was leaving, being taken away, and his only feeling for me was one of complete love. Chester loved me fully, and he expressed his love for me in that instant. It was a great compliment, and I am holding that compliment and that feeling of his love with me. Why should I give it up to Gene? I never like Gene anyway. We have met numerous times. Twice I did it with Gene, and he paid well, but I have no feeling for him. He is too independent. Too American, and too stupid for my taste. Gene does not know how to make love. Why should I share anything with Gene?

Gene

OK, I've read the above comments by Frances, and what can I say? Everybody is entitled to think what they like. It doesn't matter much in the end anyway. It's been three weeks and still no sign of Chester, Natale has notified the police, which is always a serious error, in my book. But the police haven't come up with anything. I don't think they're too worried about it. There are thousands, literally thousands of such cases every year in this country. People are just disappearing: getting abducted, inducted, and conducted every day to parts unknown. How many are living on the streets? Out of cars? How many are in the prisons? How many are dying of cancer because of the pollution? There are a lot of statistics they don't want you to know.

But Chester? I can't figure how Chester could be so careless as to just get lost. Chester wouldn't do that. It's only something evil and subterfuge that would try to hurt a sweet soul like Chester, a soul that just likes to play music and walk in the mountains. No, it's something serious and sinister that got hold of Chester. I figure the FBI may have him. Because Chester possesses the secret of reincarnation. And the FBI may figure they can use reincarnated agents or astral bodies to accomplish difficult or risky missions. Like to go back in time and the whatnot. The FBI is into things like that. They're into everything. They have agents all over the place. Some of them could be reincarnated souls. Why not?

Chester is a reincarnated soul. I knew that all along. I'm not sure if he himself knows that, or if he knows what his first life - or previous lives - actually were, but he's aware that he's not here for the first time. It's just a feeling that you have, a look that you have. And Chester's got it.

I got it too, although I can't tell you who or where I was in previous incarnations. What I do know is that I've been alive on this earth before, and that I'm just killing time, just floating, on this particular go-round. I'm spiraling, though. Spiraling up. My eyes will see the glory of the coming of the Lord, etc.

Of course, the FBI theory is only a hypothesis. But we have to pursue every lead, as they say in Scotland Yard. We're checking out all possibilities. We're short on clues, though. Chester left no trace, no indication of anything. Natale says that she's heard about a young guy called Carlos who lives in town. Now, this Carlos is a drug dealer. I've heard of him. He sells cocaine mostly - which I never touch anymore. I just smoke weed. Carlos apparently knows Chester from before. Perhaps from Chester's previous life? And here's the kicker: Carlos knew Tony. And it was Carlos that Tony was working for when he got shot down in LA. Davie knows something about it too, and Davie don't want to talk. That's how I'm putting it together. The salient fact here is that it's the people who knew Tony that don't want to talk: Davie and Andrea. They knew Tony, and they probably know how and why Tony got killed. And they're not talking. Now, I know Davie a bit, and for him not to talk is significant. Something is definitely fishy with this Carlos.

Myself, I think Chester is being held by this Carlos, in a joint operation with the FBI. But where do they have him? All I can tell you is I'm going to find out.

Carlos Peretz

OK, so you think it's strange for a guy like me, a criminal (I admit it, I'm a drug dealer, or rather a former drug dealer) to be making entries into this book. And all what I can say in my way of response is the saying "let he who is without sins cast the first stone." First of all, I'm reformed, out of the drug business, and I am strictly legitimate at this point of time. Secondly, there's a lot of people - like people in the music business, and especially there's a lot of people in the movie business - who have more stuff up their noses than I ever did. It's only that you don't know about them. Believe me, my hermanos and hermanas, there are a lot of real heavy users up in the hills, the famed and fabled Hollywood Hills. And you show me a user who ain't a dealer, and I'll just say that you just don't know that he's dealing. It's a rare bird that doesn't deal. And once you get into junkies and dealers, and you realize the extent of the phenomenon, well, you get my point. But let me please to continue. I hope I have sufficiently explained my point and justified myself, although I don't have to justify myself to no man.

Actually, I came into the drug business by chance. I was in New York, living in Jackson Heights, Queens, going to college there at St. John's. My father was a diplomat at the U.N. And he set me and my brother up in an apartment, so we could go to school and not bother him and my mother, since they was all busy with his career, going to dinners and theatre openings all the time, having guests over. Me and my brother, Pablito, we both started snorting a bit, just for fun, 'cause we was like partying all the time. I mean all the time, 'cause it was really absolute back then. And before you knew it, we was dealing. You see, it was so easy for us, what with my father's diplomatic license plates and my easy passport and customs, and we was making some sweet money. It was a couple of years before we got busted for the first time. The arrest was no sweat. We were out of the can that same night. But as far as Pappi was concerned, we was finished, cut off, caput. He pulled the plug on the apartment and all the privileges.

Pablito went back to Bogata with his tail between his legs, like they say. Only I stayed on in New York. By myself. And guess how I was paying my rent. And then I moved to L.A. And then eventually out here to Vegas. Which is how I met Tony and Chester. And although it is all very bizarre how it came to happen, all I can tell you is that Chester changed my life. He turned me around, 180 degrees, he straightened me out. And I am thankful to Chester. The son of a bitch stole like sixty grand from me, although it wasn't really his fault I don't think. Still he ripped me for sixty G. I forgive him because I love him. And because, like I say, he saved my life.

I believe you were told about it in the first book about how I was going to shoot Chester. It was simple business, something that had to be done. In the drug business you can't to let nobody mess with you or diss you in any what way. So I had no choice in the matter of hitting him. I had the safety off the gun, and was easing into it, putting that sweet squeeze on the trigger. You see, I had taken him to some deserted place out in the desert. But then the bastard asked me for a drink of water. He stunned me with that question. I didn't know what to do. I was like on ice. So, I just left him. I figured he would die out there in the desert where I left him. But the bastard walked or crawled like ten miles back to the main road and got rescued.

OK, what do I care? I'll tell you how I care. I mean I had to explain it to my boys Tummy and Julio, plus some other guys. And it all started me thinking. The thing about the glass of water is what I couldn't get out of my head. Why did he ask for a glass of water? What a question like that does is to turn somebody into a real person. Now, I suddenly discover myself in the act of killing someone who is real. And what for? It shook me up. It really did. And after a couple of days of thinking (actually I was high on grass and coke for all that time, without any kind of sleep, I just couldn't sleep) I decided to get out of the drug business. First I bought into a strip club in LA, and I wound up with sole ownership. It's a very good business. You might call it illicit or dirty, and I might have to agree with you. But at the time, it seemed quite legit. You see, I'm giving it up too. It's all Chester's influence. I'm going back to college. Can you believe that? Here in Vegas. I'm enrolled for next term, and I start in two weeks. Business administration, that's me. Mr. Straight. I have to go buy some pencils and notebooks like at the Office Depot. Chester said he'd go with me, when he gets back from LA. That's where he is, by the way. In LA.

There's a little job he's going to do for me. A favor. Something I'm going to pay him real good for. Meantime, it's Chester who's paid me. He returned a balled-up, old, hundred dollar bill that I gave to his girl Andrea. Actually, I gave it to her nice and clean, but she must've balled it up, like she got insulted by my giving her a big tip. Chester said that this'll be like his encore performance for me. Me too. I'm together with Chester in this bizarre kind of way, and I understand enough and seen enough to know that being together with Chester is not your ordinary type of thing. God knows, between him and Tony, they almost drove me crazy - not to mention Willie, who Chester told me last night is also tied in with them. And I can dig that too.

Chester was my nemesis, my curse, my bad luck charm. And now here I am hoping and praying that he's my angel. What do I care? I have to take a chance anyway. If it doesn't work out, then it's Chester who takes the consequences. So, we're rolling the dice, like they say here in Lost Wages. If I win, I'm out of all this shit. This is my last job, my encore performance. I know you don't believe me, but it's the truth. I may be a criminal, but I don't lie.

Natale the Detective

Last night Gene and I went to see this fellow Carlos. What a slimeball. What a creep! I refuse to believe that Chester could have had anything to do with him. But all the evidence is pointing in that direction. Carlos is obviously a criminal type. His whole presentation, his behavioral pattern is lifted straight out of the sociopath section of a standard psych 1 textbook: no conscience, no compunctions about lying, no real feelings. Naturally, he told us with a straight face that he knows nothing of Chester. In fact, initially he stated emphatically that he had never even heard of anyone called Chester. "Who's this Chester man. Who's this Chester?" he kept repeating. It's just amazing how easily lies come to that kind of personality. I was having a lot of trouble with it, you know, controlling my anger. But luckily Gene, who was with me, knew how to handle him. Gene is quite clever in his way, quite developed.

Gene listened to him very patiently and then asked, "What if there really was a guy named Chester, and he was in Las Vegas, where do you figure he'd go to?"

And Carlos responded, "If I had a name like Chester, I'd get out of this city altogether, like right away, like to another city, like maybe to Los Angeles or San Bernardino or somewheres."

Gene then asked him: "And how long would you stay there? Like, if you were Chester, would you come back, or would you stay in San Bernardino for the rest of your life?"

"What you talkin' rest of my life? Chester, he'll do what he wants to do. And, let me tell you sometin' that maybe you don't know, or like maybe you definitely don't know. And that is that if I was Chester - 'cause we're only talking make-believe-like over here - if I was Chester, then maybe I'd be in heaven already, or someplace like that. Like my life wouldn't be like no normal kind of life. It would be up in the clouds, high up there, man. Do you understand me, man? Like once he's gone, he's gone. Don't worry about that Chester dog no more, 'cause it ain't none of your business anyhow."

That's how we left it. Gene said that Carlos is right. We ought to just forget about it for now. Gene did say that he was going to talk to Chester's friend Davie to see if Davie knew anyone in LA who could help. This Davie is another of Chester's acquaintances whom I do not understand at all. He's a very old man, a bit demented, very talkative, and somewhat dissociative. Most of what he says is sheer nonsense. I spent several hours sitting next to him one time at one of the lounge clubs Willie was playing at, and this Davie told stupid, off-color jokes the entire time. That is, whenever he didn't have his hands on me. The old man is an idiot. I don't think he can read. I believe he's dyslexic. But Chester told me that Davie is a genius, or enlightened, or some word like that. Chester likes him very much, and I don't know why. He even said one time that Davie is "a prince". Can you imagine that? Davie is clearly a narcissistic personality, and I must say I feel little sympathy for him. I told that to Chester. I believe I referred to Davie as a "dirty old man", but Chester laughed and responded, "Oh, no. Davie's a prince."

Davie

Well, they called me in to help them with Chester. "They" meaning Gene and Natale, Chester's friends. She's a real good-lookin' girl, but Gene spoke to me on his own. He come over to the bar around five, maybe six o'clock in the afternoon, a quiet time, usually, for me, and he said that if I could help in any way to locate Chester, etcetera, etcetera, and so forth. Chester, Willie, Tony. Whatever. The guy's missin' again. I told 'em I couldn't help, but all the time Gene's talkin', I'm thinkin' how I still know some people in Los Angeles from the time I used to live there. Because I used to live in West LA off of Sepulveda Blvd, as well as when Mildred and myself had a very nice little apartment in North Hollywood, but then we had to move out on account of the mice, but that's neither here nor there. I tell ya, that was some story with the mice, though. I'll tell you that one another time.

So, what was I sayin'?.... Yeah, I have a couple friends in LA, and they owe me a favor or two, and they'll let me know the score if they hear of anything. Because if I could do anything for Chester, I'd do it at the drop of a hat. I don't know why, but I would. I suppose I've known the kid for a long while already. I've known him under a whole handful of names already. To tell you the truth, I don't even know who the heck he is. But I can tell you this: I love him. He's a real swell guy. And, so, if there's anything that I can do for him, I'll do it. That's the kind of guy I am. Davie Goldstein is always there for his friends. I could tell you a number of stories - I could write a book myself, not just write in this stupid diary book that no one's ever gonna read. The point is I could tell true stories about all the times I put it on the line for other fellas, and I could also tell a whole bunch of stories about how other guys put it on the line for me. It would all be true. You see, I could always take care of myself. In those days you had to, you had to be able to take care of yourself. In Chicago, back in the old days. Did I tell you I come from Chicago? Anyhow, the more things change, the more they stay the same. That's what my mother used to say, God bless her. May she rest in peace, she was right.

Chester Has the Last Word

This will be the final chapter in this diary book, because these are the last pages in the notebook. I'm out of paper. Firstly I want to put to rest all fears that I am dead. I am still among the living, albeit as a pure spirit now. My body got shot full of bullets and was left on a side street near Vanowen Blvd in the Valley. But I'm out on the beach right now, and I am fine.

I succeeded in concluding Carlos' business, and I hope he straightens himself out. I sold two kilos of heroin for him, and the check is in the mail. Really, I put the cash into a cardboard box and mailed it via first-class postage. There was a very long line at the post office. You see, there was some trouble with the actual delivery of the drugs, which is why Carlos had me do it. Two kids, Jonesy and Black Spider, who drive around in BMW/SUVs all day met me at a strip club in the San Fernando Valley, which is where I picked up the heroin from Tummy, Carlos' man. Tummy and I are old friends.

Tummy almost fell over when he saw me. I walked up to the strip club entrance and saw him at the window. He's the bouncer there, and Carlos promised to give Tummy his half interest in the club once he gets the cash, which should be sometime next week if the US Postal service holds up. Tummy staggered when he saw me and bumped into a cardboard marquee.

He kept repeating "So you're the guy Carlos sent? It's bizarre. It's bizarre, man. Really bizarre, man. Man, this is really bizarre."

Tummy likes the words bizarre and absolutely. He said it was "absolutely important" that I have a couple of lap dances before we do any business. As bouncer, Tummy gets full privileges with the girls, which is quite a perk, I suppose. Tummy was introducing me to April, and April was pushing herself up against me, when I saw out of the corner of my eye the familiar bulkhead silhouette of my buddy Davie Goldstein, who was sitting at the bar having a Coke. Davie gave me a wink which only I could see. Davie had been waiting for me all day. Afterwards he told me that it was a good thing I arrived when I did. "Otherwise", he said, "another turn of that little girl dancing naked on my lap would' a killed me!"

Tummy led me into a back room, past a corridor where several of the girls were putting on perfume, combing their hair, etc, getting dressed or undressed to go onstage. The hallway was cold and dark. The only lighting was from purple and red strob lights. We passed though some parted red curtains into the back room, which was a bedroom of sorts. Tummy pulled two plastic Ralph's shopping bags from under a bed. The bags were heavy with sealed baggies of heroin. He plopped them onto the bed, a large waterbed, and they bounced and bobbed up and down comically. Tummy grinned and hugged me. I gave him Carlos' message about the split of the business. Tummy kept hugging me, he was so happy.

Suddenly there were three big Black guys with ski hats on - and Uzis pointed at us. They had been standing behind some curtain, or they had come in through some back door. It was so dark they could have come out of the walls. Anyway, we were taken by surprise. The Black Spider guy lifted the bags off the bed with a wide grin.

"Thank you very much, fellas. We'll come back for a lap dance a bit later, perhaps later tonight. What do you say, gentlemen? This is a gentlemen's club, ain't it? I tell ya'll, I don't get it why they called it a gentlemen's club, when all it got in it is ho's and these here two pussies. They ain't no gentlemen, neider. They din' bring me my money that Carlos owes me. They din' bring no extra powder! They din'......."

Spider man was floored by a blow to the head. A metal pole rammed into Jonesy's stomach and Tummy attacked the third guy. In a moment, it was already over. Davie grimaced and said. "How yer doin' Chester? Come on. Let's get the heck out of here. And no more lap dances!"

Davie's body dominated the room, as he leaned over to rummage through the clothes of the fallen hoodlums.

"Here!" he said as he lifted a thick packet of money from the pants pocket of Black Spider. "This must be yer money."

He tossed the packet to me, and we made for the back door, stepping over the crumpled, unconscious bodies - as well as piles of videos, which had fallen onto the floor in the melee. Tummy stayed behind to "clean up". Davie and I walked briskly down a dirty alleyway over to his old Cadillac, which was parked at the corner.

When he got to the car Davie said, "Jeezus Chester, that sure was somethin' back there. Man, did you see that guy go down when I hit 'im with that broomstick? It was a nice metal broomstick, or whatever the hell it was. I shoulda kept it….. Well, where do you wanna go? I'm going straight back ta Vegas. I'm workin, tomorra. Your people been worried 'bout cha, Chester, but if you wez smart, you'd lay low for a coupla days, maybe a week or two. I got a friend in Barstow, maybe, that could take ya in for a week or so....."

I refused his offer. I wanted to walk. I hugged big Davie and kissed him on both cheeks goodbye. And headed toward Sherman Way.

I figured I wanted to stay in LA a couple of days. I had promised Willie that I would. When you're in the kind of situation I'm in, what with my reincarnations, second lives, and spiritual meanderings, you begin to feel invulnerable. But I had just been lucky, that's all. And my luck ran out a just a few moments later......

Well, first, I found a post office and mailed a parcel full of money to Carlos. When I came out, though, just as I turned onto Sherman Way Blvd, I got shot. I was hit by twenty or thirty bullets. I saw the side window of a big fancy SUV roll down. And then I saw a series of flashes, and felt the burning in my gut. Well, that's all I remember.

I'm here at the beach now. Clearly, there's something that always draws me to the beach. The waves are cold at my feet, and although I don't have corporeal feet, strictly speaking, it feels wonderful. The lines created on the sand with every wave, the shifting curves, the pull of the water rushing back to the ocean, the spray from the salt water, the sunlight, the roar of the surf - all echo within me now.

www.ingramcontent.com/pod-product-compliance
Lightning Source LLC
Chambersburg PA
CBHW032212030726
47494CB00020B/995